T0246352

WITH THEIR HEARTS IN THEIR BOOTS

JEAN-PIERRE MARTINET

WITH THEIR HEARTS IN THEIR BOOTS

followed by

AT THE BACK OF THE COURTYARD ON THE RIGHT

FOREWORD BY WILLIAM BOYLE
TRANSLATED BY ALEX ANDRIESSE

WAKEFIELD PRESS / CAMBRIDGE, MASSACHUSETTS

This translation © 2024 Wakefield Press

Wakefield Press, P.O. Box 425645, Cambridge, MA 02142

Originally published as *Ceux qui n'en menent pas large* in 1986.
© le dilettante, 1986, renewed 2008

All rights reserved. No part of this book may be reproduced in any form by any electronic or mechanical means (including photocopying, recording, or information storage and retrieval) without permission in writing from the publisher.

This book was set in Garamond Premier Pro and Helvetica Neue Pro by Wakefield Press. Printed and bound by Versa Press in the United States of America.

ISBN: 978-1-962728-02-7

Available through D.A.P./Distributed Art Publishers
75 Broad Street, Suite 630
New York, New York 10004
Tel: (212) 627-1999
Fax: (212) 627-9484

10   9   8   7   6   5   4   3   2   1

CONTENTS

FOREWORD

Jean-Pierre Martinet is a mystery to me. If I'm being honest, that's been part of the draw. Sure, the work comes first—and I've responded very strongly to the little bit I've been able to read—but the fact that his books have largely been swallowed up in the big nowhere of time has helped to create something of a blind pursuit on my part, searching dark alleys for a scrap or a fragment, piecing together a life and career through half-heard whispers.

But let me back up for a minute.

In late January 2017, I discovered Henry Vale's translation of Martinet's *The High Life*, which had been published by Wakefield Press five years earlier. Jay Gertzman, author of *Pulp According to David Goodis*, had written a brief review of it, noting that Martinet was deeply influenced by Goodis and that *The High Life* was reminiscent of *The Blonde on the Street Corner*. That was probably enough to sell me, but Gertzman went on to compare *The High Life* to Jim Thompson's *Savage Night*, Francisco Carco's *Perversity* (translated by Jean Rhys), and William Kotzwinkle's *The Fan Man*—all books I love.

Finding *The High Life* also marked my discovery of Wakefield Press, which has become one of my favorite publishers. I'm always hunting literature in translation, and it turned out—beyond Martinet—Wakefield published many writers that I either loved or would come to love. When my friend Alex Andriesse visited me the following summer, I passed *The High Life* along to him, telling him it blew me away and that it was the only book of Martinet's available in English. I didn't know much, but I knew there were at least a few other books out there. He said he'd investigate.

On several tours in France over the coming years, I would always hunt for Martinet's books on shelves. They were there—especially *Jérôme*, widely considered his masterpiece—and I even bought a couple, but I can't read French adequately and so the rest of Martinet remained unknowable to me. I'd heard he hadn't sold well in France during his lifetime but that he'd been "rediscovered" in the mid-aughts, so I expected erudite French writer and publisher and bookseller pals to know his work. Alas, almost none of them did. Only one said he'd read *Jérôme* (or, perhaps, was made to read it at university) and had found it truly disturbing.

The High Life is a book I've revisited several times over the last seven years, a slim, haunting, darkly funny novella. I'd begun to think it was all I'd ever be able to read of Martinet's work. And then I got an email one day from Alex that he was translating *With Their Hearts in Their Boots*, a late book from Martinet I'd seen passing mention of. I knew very little, other than that I was excited, both that Alex was translating the work and to simply have gained access to another piece of the puzzle.

For a sketch of Martinet's tragic life in English, Henry Vale's introduction to his translation of *The High Life* is about all there is out there. I won't go through it again, but obviously Martinet was stung by rejection and failure, both in the film and publishing worlds. After his second novel, *Jérôme*, was greeted by indifference, he used some money he came into to open a newsstand in Tours. That too failed. In the mid 1980s, at the age of forty, Martinet returned home to live with his mother in Libourne. In "The Impossible Self-Respect: Martinet, *Jérôme* and the Game of Massacre," Frédéric Sounac describes Martinet's existence with his mother in their "tomb-home" as "reclusive" and bathed in a "nauseating atmosphere." Martinet descended into alcoholism. It was during this period that he wrote *With Their Hearts in Their Boots,* which fits nicely alongside booze-soaked novels like Charles Jackson's *The Lost Weekend* and John O'Brien's *Leaving Las Vegas.* I hate to use Wikipedia as a source (and I can't find confirmation of this elsewhere, though it seems too strange and specific to make up), but apparently, during this time, Martinet's mother "roamed the cafés of Libourne, armed with a wooden pistol, shouting 'Hands up!'" and Martinet "feared the attacks of mysterious birds with a steel beak." It is difficult, then, not to imagine Martinet, drunk, writing this while deep in the throes of paranoia over these nightmare birds and then rushing to collect his mother from her mock holdups.

The plan for *With Their Hearts in the Their Boots* was for it to be a much longer novel but, at some point, Martinet—either unable or unwilling to make it the full-length book he'd once envisioned it as—published it as a novella. On paper, not much happens in *Hearts.* A washed-up actor, Georges Maman, a.k.a. "Bloody Mama," is reduced to starring in a porno film; but he can't get it up, so he goes to a dive bar and drinks and gripes, yearning for his lost love, the now successful and happily married Marie Beretta. Eventually, he meets up with an annoying old acquaintance from the film world named Dagonard, and the night plays out in a drunken haze of tension, the two men talking movies and books, scrapping and bullshitting, Maman angling for a free meal from the generous Dagonard, the possibility of Maman lashing out violently hanging over the whole encounter. The writers that Martinet references and no doubt idolizes—Goodis, Thompson (Dagonard dreams of adapting *The Nothing Man*), and Horace McCoy— make their presence known in every moment of the proceedings. The book is shot through with their brand of desperation. Maman feels like a mix of McCoy's Gloria Beatty and a typical Goodis or Thompson protagonist, existing somewhere on the verge of catastrophe and confusion, between mania and murder. It's a dark, strange, hilarious book that goes down like sweet poison.

Martinet, who worked as an assistant director at the Office de radiodiffusion-télévision française for many years, dreamed of making a film but never did. The anguish that seeps from the pores of this story no doubt comes from Martinet's own sense of longing over unrealized projects and dreams. The films he never made, the books he wrote that were immediately forgotten, the loves he lost—there is so much pain here. And humor too, of course, as a balm for that pain. Maman is a poet of hating things and people. So is Martinet. You can feel him trying to make sense of how awful and fucked up and unfair the world is. ("Doors locked on emptiness" is one of my favorite observations Maman makes as he waits to use the bathroom at the bar.) The bad guys succeed, and the good guys lose, but . . . Maman is not quite a good guy. At best, he's a disaster. (I thought several times of poet Everette Maddox's memorial plaque at the Maple Leaf Bar in New Orleans: *He was a mess.*) At worst, Maman's a crude missile of nastiness. One thing's for sure, though. He's the kind of romantic failure— a picture of Lauren Bacall on the wall of his dingy apartment—that you want to follow through the night. Imagine Martin Scorsese's *After Hours* written by some unholy combination of Goodis and McCoy, and you can start to approximate Martinet's vision here.

WILLIAM BOYLE

Andriesse's translation captures the soul of Martinet's prose, which has the timeless qualities of the best noir fiction. Hard-boiled, funny, dangerous. Cynical interiority wed to an atmosphere of dreamy desolation. Clipped sentences that punch hard. A rat-a-tat of bitter ranting. Every word, every line of dialogue, and every sad detail fueling the darkness and dread. What Martinet is doing feels deeply contemporary—Maman is a person who wants to live in movies, who desires the fantasies that burn through his imagination but who can't stop fucking up and squandering his days.

Finally, at the end of this volume, there's Martinet's "At the Back of the Courtyard," a short piece on the writer Henri Calet, who had two books translated into English in the 1950s—*Monsieur Paul* and *Young Man in Paris*—but whose work is long out of print and forgotten here. Martinet originally published it in 1978 in *Subjectif*, where he also published *The High Life* in 1979. The editors at French publishing house Le Dilettante added the Calet piece to the second edition of *With Their Hearts in Their Boots* after Martinet had died. Weirdly, it functions as a sort of coda, so much so that—when I first read it—I thought it was just a challenging final section, an attempt at an oblique and illuminating ending. Calet was a writer Martinet felt a great affinity for, a writer virtually inaccessible to those of us confined to English, whose books are by all accounts brutal. One of Martinet's proudest accomplishments as a reviewer was to bring attention back to Calet at a point when he'd long been neglected in France. Many of Calet's novels are now available in Gallimard's Imaginaire series.

I hope this new translation marks the beginning of folks truly starting to discover Martinet here in America. Selfishly, I'd love to see more of his books in English—especially his first two novels, *Somnolence* (a death-haunted, alcoholic *Alice in Wonderland*, to hear Andriesse describe it) and *Jérôme*. I wonder how Martinet will land with readers now—if he's too hard, too angry, too twisted—but I hope people will be drawn to the romantic yearning and desperation that makes this short novel hum like a classic paranoid noir. The world has beat up on Maman, he's lost in all ways, battered, a dour guide through the lower depths of hell on earth.

William Boyle

WITH THEIR HEARTS IN
THEIR BOOTS

After a while it gets so bad you want to stop
the whole business.

David Goodis
Retreat from Oblivion

Maman was looking at the sky but no one up there was looking at him, he was sure of that. There was no fooling him. He had the true professional's instinct. No light on him, not the least little spotlight, nothing. Nobody was moving behind the clouds. The stagehands were silent for once. There wasn't even the sound of the camera or the squeaking of the dolly. No clapstick for action and no clapstick for cut. A real desert up there. The script had split. The director too. The cinematographer had left off directing the light, that's why the stagecraft looked so broken up, so incomplete. Try as he might to be reasonable about it, the absence of staging made Maman nervous. He longed to disappear into a movie theater, any movie theater, just to forget for a while how fucked up and lousy life was, but he was so broke he decided to keep the little bit of money he had left to knock back a few beers. Between one drug and the other, he had to choose. In Paris, near the end of November, when it was just starting to get cold, he almost always had this horrible feeling of abandonment, but this year it was worse than ever. A real shitshow. He pushed through the door of the first dive he came to and leaned on the bar. The bartender took his time coming, and Maman crushed a hardboiled egg on the counter just to make a bit of noise, or to calm his nerves, he wasn't sure. Anyhow, he felt weird. Even weirder than this time last winter. That old pair of pincers with its curved jaws was slowly closing on his neck. For a good long while now the whole sorry mess had been a torment. Several months at least. He'd almost forgotten it, truth be told. He probably shouldn't have stayed cooped up at home so long after that porno shoot. Being alone like that had wound up making him a little loonier than the next guy, no doubt. He thought about Marie Beretta and crushed another hardboiled egg on the counter. Marie. Marie. Their paths had diverged, that's all. Just a matter of paths diverging. No reason to make a fuss, Maman told himself. Yet he could feel the tears welling in his eyes. Beretta Marie. It sounded completely idiotic when you put it that way. No magic at all. As bleak as a birth certificate or a social security form. Marie was history. Bye-bye life, bye-bye love. Nothing worth crying over. Mechanically he crushed another hardboiled egg on the counter, then another. Nothing like it for calming the nerves.

"You're not going to eat them?"

Maman jumped, as if he'd been jarred out of the deepest sleep in the dead of night. It was his neighbor at the bar, a little old man in a cap who must have been on his sixth glass of rosé. His voice quavered slightly.

"Not going to eat what?"

"The eggs. You're going to break them like that and not eat them?"

This guy was spoiling for a fight for sure. At any rate, he didn't like his face. And that little cap . . . Exactly the kind of old prick who chortles over the jokes in *Le Hérisson*.[1] But Maman had made up his mind not to be dragged into anything. His nerves were fried, and it was no time to crack. Marie wouldn't have liked it. No, certainly not. So he made an effort to control himself.

"No, I'm not going to eat them. I'm going to break them and not eat them. And that's how it's going to be. But don't you worry, I am going to pay for them. At least if the bartender ever shows up . . ."

The man in the little cap didn't seem the least bit satisfied by the explanations of his neighbor at the bar and belabored the point:

"I beg your pardon, sir, but if you don't mind my asking, why are you breaking those eggs if you don't intend to eat them? It's obscene. Think of Ethiopia, sir. You ought to be ashamed."

Same old story everywhere you went. The world was lousy with people who stuck their noses in where they didn't belong. Professional pains in the neck, human rights fanatics, hankering for universal love, intoxicated by the fraternity of man! And sermonizers to boot.

Relentless, as soon as the opportunity presented itself to show off their beautiful souls, their beautiful little throbbing and generous souls. Nowadays they might disguise themselves as retired taxi drivers or pikers crazy for the ponies. Who could you trust? Nothing looked like anything anymore. Maman wanted to grab the little old man by the lapels and chuck him out into the street, but he just crushed another hardboiled egg in his fist. He cut himself on a piece of shell, but so lightly he found it almost pleasurable.

"I hate eggs, sir, that's all there is to it. I hate them deeply. And I don't give a rat's ass about Ethiopia."

Marie would be pleased if she could see him now. This was the way she liked him—calm, just a little insolent when somebody was trying to start something. The sort of guy you see in Westerns. Maman was proud of himself. He turned around to face the room. Even if Marie Beretta wasn't there, maybe he'd at least get a round of applause. But no. Nobody seemed to be paying him any attention. Still, he relished the line. It had been damn well delivered. He wondered where he'd got it from. "I don't give a rat's ass about eggs. And I detest Ethiopia." That wasn't the wording exactly, but it caught the spirit of the thing. Always these fucking problems with memory. A real nuisance for an actor to be incapable of retaining a single line verbatim anymore. He couldn't remember exactly when he started singing "J'ai la mémoire qui flanche,"[2] but it was a long time ago, he was sure of that. Marie had already long since left him. Gently. The way one leaves a sick child. Like most pretty women, she hated losers. She could smell them from ten kilometers off. It hadn't taken her long to see that Georges Maman was always going to be hopeless at making his way in life, despite his incontestable talent as an actor. Feeling no call to be a sister of mercy, she'd found her salvation in flying the coop. Anyway, for the moment, Maman was happy as a clam to have shut down the little old man in the cap. Eggs! Ethiopia! Etcetera! The whole damn thing! In one fell swoop! He'd slunk off without further ado, the tactless humanist! He'd have to tell Marie the story, it was one she'd appreciate, no doubt about it. The annoying thing, though, was that nobody, absolutely nobody in this foul saloon, recognized him, Maman, Georges Maman. Didn't any of these people go to the theater or the movies, or ever watch television? Hard to credit. The pincers had moved, little by little, and were now gripping his hips. All things considered, it was better than the neck. Less suffocating.

"And for monsieur?"

Finally, they were seeing to him. The bartender stared him down with almost embarrassing insistence. Maybe he was just trying to put a name to the face. That was it. The guy must have his name on the tip of his tongue, and he was all tied up in knots about it. Lapse of memory. He knew the feeling well.

"A demi. Easy on the foam."

Maybe, too, he was awed to find himself face-to-face with an actor. In a joint as crummy as this one, it must not be an everyday occurrence, seeing famous performers plonking themselves down at the bar like this, without affectation, elbow to elbow with the regulars. At any rate, Maman wouldn't say no to an autograph. His whole career he'd never said no to anyone asking for an autograph, and he wasn't going to start now. He'd always considered it part of the job. Stuck-up wasn't his style. He'd remained simple, in spite of his failures.

"Maman . . ."

The bartender's eyes widened. "Mama, is it? Now you think I'm your mother? Really, buddy, things aren't looking too good for you. First you perpetrate a massacre of hardboiled eggs, and now . . . I'm tempted to toss you out on your ear. Sainte-Anne's not too far down the line. You get off at Glacière."[3]

"Take it easy. I just meant my name's Maman. Georges Maman, the actor. I thought you were trying to put a name to the face and I just wanted to help you out . . ."

The bartender swept the hardboiled egg debris off the counter with a furious flick of the wrist and, muttering, pulled a glass.

"There's your demi and keep a lid on it. OK?"

Maman bowed his head.

"OK."

Too much foam, of course. It trickled down the rim. It always trickled down the rim. Nobody could be bothered to pull a demi correctly in this shit-stain town. A bunch of assholes, and the bartenders above all. Was there even a drop of beer in all this foam? A crushed slug, drowning in slobber—that's what the barkeep had served him. Nobody would ever serve Delon such a ghastly beer. Maman drained the glass in one gulp.

"Give me another. One with less slobber, if possible . . ."

On the fourth demi, he felt a little better. He dared to look the bartender in the face again.

"Honest, though, you never heard of me?"

"Never. But the thing is I go to the movies all the time, you know. If Depardieu came in for a drink, I'd recognize him straight off, no problem. Or Belmondo. I'm no dumber than the next guy. But Maman, no. Never heard of him. And anyway, that's no name for an actor. Either you're screwing with me or you're totally out of your gourd. Either way, it's not my problem. Counting the eggs, that'll be forty-three francs."

Maman threw a wadded-up fifty-franc bill on the counter.

"Careful with that now, it's my last one . . ."

The bartender looked disgusted as he unfolded the bill. "And broke to boot," he heard him grumble. Just like that, he burned with shame. This guy despised him, he could feel it. Probably he'd noticed Maman's shirt collar was none too clean and his jacket well on its way to ruin. Nothing to do with the chic scruffiness in vogue, just skulking poverty. He looked down at his shoes: Truly pathetic, not quite Chaplinesque, but getting there. Good thing Marie couldn't see him in this condition! Maybe— what a nightmare!—she might have taken pity on him. She might have slipped him a hundred-franc bill. Except . . . Pity and charity weren't exactly Beretta Marie's style. Nothing to fear on that front. "Still," Maman said to himself, "I must have stayed cooped up in my room too long, that has to be why everybody looks so weird to me, why they all freak me out . . ." The pain was on the move again. It wasn't like being tortured with pincers anymore, but like a billy club steadily coming down on his neck. The nauseating rhythm of a metronome. Tick-tock. Tick-tock. Right, left, right, left. A graceless, perfectly stupid rhythm as mind-numbing as a disco tune. For a moment, Maman stared at an invisible pendulum in the air. It swung to the rhythm of his pain, and he followed it with eyes.

"Where's the phone?"

"In the back on the right. No tokens. But somebody's in there right now."

"No big deal, I'll wait."

Truth be told, what he wanted more than anything was to urinate, but he didn't dare ask the bartender where the toilets were. He'd already called him broke. He wouldn't scruple to charge him extra for the simple right to relieve his bladder. For some time now the most innocuous acts had been getting terribly complicated: buying newspapers or cigarettes, phoning friends, crossing a street without getting run over. Collecting unemployment above all. Yet almost every actor did it, and he himself had gone through the selfsame drudgery for years without batting an eye. Anyway, it was because he'd already used up his benefits, unable to submit enough working hours for the current year, that he'd wound up accepting, out of desperation, a small role in that goddamn porno. The cruel god of the Assédic had gotten him at last.[4] He'd immolated himself, and for peanuts at that! The few lines he had to say had been scratched, and he'd found himself buck naked atop a girl he didn't even desire. She was pretty enough, though, despite her empty, almost dead eyes, but really, her breasts were too big. He could never stand big bosoms, even when he was little. It was a real phobia. Humongous udders terrified him. Run for your life! Suddenly he was overcome by an uncontrollable panic. He could never bring himself to fuck this girl in front of all these people. It was a small, bare-bones crew, but still, no, nothing doing. Even in private, he couldn't have pulled it off. He'd tried closing his eyes and thinking with all his might of Marie. Marie. Marie. Her eternally adolescent body. All that did was cause him pain, intolerable pain. The girl, under him, was getting impatient: "So is this, like, ever going to happen?"

Luckily the two cameras weren't rolling yet. Mouliane, the director, knew his job like the back of his hand. An old stager, a sort of Raoul Walsh of porn. Nothing panicked him, especially not something this banal. Shooting a sequence like this, he knew that most of the time it was better not to call action—that the important thing was to start rolling once the actors began to forget about the presence of the camera.

"Is this going to happen today, or what?

Maman wasn't thinking of today or tomorrow, but of yesterday and the day before yesterday, and the days before that too, all the squandered days. The girl's voice was vulgar, slightly raspy. Her breath stank, but he couldn't nail down the odor exactly: onion, garlic sausage, mackerel filets in mustard sauce? Dog food? Rabbit-flavor Whiskas? Poultry kidneys brought to you by Fido? Hard to say. He'd often shared cans of dog food with an old mutt he'd loved way back when, a mutt who died of grief after Marie split, and they all had pretty much the same odor, the taste hardly differed from brand to brand. So it was rather tricky to ascertain. The ways were dark and the days difficult. "Marie. Marie. Marie full of grace," Maman kept murmuring, not registering that the girl must have thought he was a wacko. "Marie. What a funny path I've taken to reach you!" At

JEAN-PIERRE MARTINET

any rate, maybe his partner had digestive troubles. Or else she was starting to rot from the inside out. Yes, that was entirely possible. Her viscera and all that—slowly. A heap of entrails. He felt like throwing up. Holy hell, what a lousy job. Better to kick the bucket than work a job like this. He'd never make a career of it. Really too disgusting. Mouliane kept his cool. He was so used to this kind of malfunction, especially with first-timers. Rule of thumb: Buck them up, don't drag them through the mud. These people were doing difficult work, work that was really no fun day in, day out, and they deserved respect, at least as much respect as other people, who thought they were earning their living with dignity and were merely humiliating themselves a little more each day. Mouliane knew there was no such thing as dignity, not in show business and not in any other business either. Generalized prostitution. No reason to lift your eyes or meet another person's gaze. A suffocating whorehouse. Not a man who didn't walk with his head down. Nothing but slaves who think they're free, prisoners who don't even have the courage to try making a break for it.

"Let's take a breather, boys and girls, and we'll get the next sequence set up. Maman, you're free for the day. And don't worry, man, tomorrow will be better."

But the next day, on set, Maman was nowhere to be found. The producers called his home number several times to no avail. He stayed curled up in bed, hiding under the covers for several days, stuffed with sleeping pills.

He kept trying to tell himself he was nowhere near ready to accept a career in porn—not realizing that competition in the business was stiff, or that Mouliane had only brought him on out of friendship—but nothing helped. He would rather die of hunger or take a walk-on part— the ultimate comedown for an actor who had, after all, played a few important roles at the start of his career. He kept trying to gauge the exact extent of the disaster, but he couldn't help now and then, as he drifted viscously in and out of consciousness, relishing his misfortune and wallowing in his grief.

And anyway, sure enough, the restrooms were occupied. Same old story. There was no room anywhere. Everything was always occupied. The metro packed. The castings complete even before they'd begun. Even when you went to piss, every spot was taken. Maybe he should pay in advance, or get his relatives involved? In November, in Paris, it was worse than usual. The first cold weather shrank everybody's bladder, and the rush was on. Tea drinkers and beer drinkers came to blows over access to the urinals. There were even injuries sometimes, the police had to be called. In general, he avoided getting embroiled in these quarrels, which he found degrading. Yet that evening Maman wasn't in the mood to be patient. The four demis he'd downed in haste, nerves on edge, had bloated his bladder to the size of a soccer ball. He could feel it now turning into a hot-air balloon, swollen with helium. Holy hell, he was going to explode right there, in a flash, pow! guts flying everywhere, what a pathetic way to go, nobody would remember him, they'd put his remains in a garbage bag, and there's the exit, good riddance, not even three lines in the papers. Who would weep for Maman, if he was no longer there to feel sorry for himself? He tried and tried, but he couldn't imagine. Certainly not Marie, anyway. She was cold and calculating. She'd never held anybody dear except numero uno. A real bitch. Not his fellow actors either. Far from it. Even if the late-Georges-Maman-to-be wasn't a very troublesome rival, it was still a free spot, up for grabs. There was so much unemployment in the profession. *The show must go on.* You've got to be kidding me. It was more like a stampede: nothing but pushing and shoving and trampling all around! The important thing was to show up before anybody else so as not to miss out on the final moments of the party no matter what the cost, no mercy for the injured or those who fell along the way, it was worse than the dance marathons in the US in the thirties. A fucked-up world and a world fucked up. You had to climb as high as possible, crushing the wounded all piled in their heap, just to breathe in the last breath of oxygen. Chop-chop! Higher! Higher and higher! And then you saw the light. Which is to say you saw nothing at all. Just these closed, demoralizing doors: Ladies; Gentlemen. Four double-locked doors in all. Ten good minutes Maman had been standing there, jigging from foot to foot. But what could they be contriving in there? Were they shooting up, or what? If they were all sufferers of chronic constipation, why didn't they just go see a doctor? He gave each door two hard kicks.

"Hey! I've been waiting out here an hour! You could think just a little about someone other than yourselves!"

No reply. Maybe they were all dead. Or else there was nobody in there, and the doors were just locked. That was it. Doors locked on emptiness. Locked from the inside, by nobody. They were clearly marked as restrooms, but it was an illusion, a sort of special effect. A trap? Four doors and behind them nothing, no one. Georges Maman found the thought unbearable. The pincers closed again, noiselessly, on his neck. He wanted to start screaming, but he settled for biting his hand violently, till it bled. Then he burst out laughing and headed for the phone booth. It was so simple. He wondered why he hadn't thought of it earlier. By some miracle, the booth was vacant. The sinks were risky, they might catch him there, but in here who would suspect him, his face to the wall, holding the receiver in one hand and, with the other, discreetly relieving his bladder? It was glorious. It had been an eternity since he felt so good. Almost happy, he might say, if the word hadn't meant something else to him. Not like those little negative pleasures, where it was just a matter of suffering being replaced by the absence of suffering, briefly giving you back your taste for life. Not a zest, but a taste. A little, at any rate. Just a little. Just what it took. The bare minimum, let's face it. And well below the minimum, to be completely frank. But at least it was that. It was a start. Better than nothing. The annoying thing, now that his bladder was no longer torturing him, was that he was thinking about Marie again. The pain was far more violent, and even similar, curiously, to the anxiety triggered by the sight of those locked doors with no one behind them, he was sure of it. He dialed her number, so feverishly that he had to start over several times. But it was busy. It was always busy. To tell the truth, he didn't know the first thing about this woman he'd lived with for months and months. And then, if by some miracle he had heard her voice on the other end of the line, he'd no doubt have been incapable of saying two words to her, he'd be so choked with emotion. He would have hung up immediately, in a full-on panic. He thought, suddenly, of the light in the Grands Boulevards in early winter, when the darkness begins to fall, and, in the space of less than a second, it was as if Marie Beretta were standing there beside him. Then, just as quickly, he found himself alone again, sloshing in his own piss. He redialed the number a good dozen times to no avail. And once again the door slammed in his face. Sometimes he felt like he'd spent his whole life waiting before a row of locked doors, in a dark hallway. All those wasted years. It was enough to make you weep with rage. He pounded his fist against the wall, then laced into the phone, hammering it over and over. He hadn't even registered that somebody was waiting on the other side of the glass door. When he noticed the man's silhouette, he felt a hot flush of shame. Hopefully he hadn't seen him pissing. It would have been useless to explain that the four restrooms were locked and there was nothing else for it, nobody'd ever believe him, they'd think he was a nutcase, perhaps a complaint might even be lodged against him. The bartender already seemed less than thrilled with the way he'd massacred the hardboiled eggs ... Maman gently opened the door of the booth and gave the man a faint smile: "You must excuse me, but I haven't been able to reach the party I'm trying to call ... And I sort of lost my temper. You know how it is ..."

The man lunged at him and gave him a violent slap on the back that almost sent him flying into the sinks.

"Hey! Hands off the head, ok?" Maman protested. This town was getting rougher and rougher. He would have been better off staying in his room, at least there he wasn't in any danger. No one was ever seriously injured falling out of bed. How he regretted setting foot outside. To stay alone and at rest. Snug. Inert. Without the slightest ambition. Just waiting for everything to pass. For it to work itself out without him.

"Maman! How ya been, mother dearest? Good to see you! Wow, it's been ages ... What have you been up to, old girl?"

Maman felt relieved. Dagonard was holding him close now, still giving him big claps on the back. He was always very expansive, Dagonard. In the trade, they called him Boxer because he acted like a big crazy dog. But Maman couldn't help thinking that most boxers were a hell of a lot more intelligent. Anyhow, Dagonard was better than some rough customer ready to break his face for behaving strangely in the phone booth.

"I'm glad to see you, Michel," Maman said half-heartedly. "I didn't recognize you in the dark."

"Maman, you old devil! Same as ever! Always such a prick! But never mind, I'm damn happy to see you anyway . . . Just a few little phone calls to make and I'm all yours. I'll buy you a demi at the bar. They have an absolutely fantastic Heineken on tap. Don't even think about refusing. Action! Haven't seen my little Maman in more than a year. That calls for a drink, doesn't it?"

Maman made a face like a guy sick to his stomach: "I've got to warn you, somebody pissed in the phone booth. It's disgusting. Really, you wonder what goes through some people's heads . . ."

"Don't worry, man, it's no big deal, nothing serious. Anyway, we'll fix it in the editing room, darling, don't be so down in the mouth. Would you believe Gaiffier changed the whole shot list for tomorrow? Ten actors to notify! No but I swear! They're getting shittier and shittier in TV, it can't go on . . . Someday I'm going to clear the hell out . . ."

While Dagonard shut himself in the booth, Maman tried to slip off. He didn't feel strong enough to bear such a thorn in his side. Truly too depressed. But he didn't get very far. Dagonard caught up with him in no time and led him back to the booth, pulling him by the collar of his jacket.

"Stay there. Wait like a good boy until I finish with my calls, and then we'll go toss one back, OK?"

"OK, Michel," Maman acquiesced, resigned. He thought he heard some vaguely threatening under-tones in Boxer's voice. At any rate, no one escaped from Dagonard. As soon as your paths crossed, it was all over, your night was ruined, or you had to be pretty clever to find an exit. When it came to holding people captive, he was unbeatable. Some took this for friendship or gen-erosity, but Maman knew, hazily, that it was something else. He studied himself in the mirror above the sinks. He tried to smile at himself, but he couldn't pull it off. "I've got an ugly mug today ... Even worse than usual." He passed one hand, slightly trembling, over a three-day beard. He in no way cared for the individual who looked at him disgustedly from the other side of the mirror. Sure wouldn't give him a ride, even if he offered a hefty sum for the lift. Yet he had no choice, nobody asked his opinion, he had to deal with this jackass till the end. Im-possible to open the door and chuck him out into the countryside.

"Hey! Mother dearest, are we ready?"

Dagonard's hand landed heavily on Maman's shoul-der, and he narrowly avoided knocking into the neon lights above the sinks. Odd to think he hadn't even seen him coming! Yet, in the mirror, he should have seen him opening the door of the phone booth and silently coming up behind him to give him another of these deranged palsy-walsy slaps. He almost asked Dagonard if he wasn't a bit of a sadist, but he bit his tongue since Boxer's reactions were so unpredictable it was best to watch your step. Anyway, for a good long while now, nothing had been working out for Maman, hence prudence. With any luck, maybe Dagonard would invite him to dinner. You never pass up a free meal when you haven't earned a cent in months and the god of the Assédic has definitively abandoned you. Old Dago, the dear old Asshole, was a picky eater, and while you couldn't be too sure you'd enjoy any fascinating conversation with him (at any rate, Maman found all conversations deadly dull), on the other hand you had a decent chance of settling in at a good table. He daydreamed about a bottle of Saint-Émilion. A grand cru classé. It would make a change from the wine he'd been buying in big 1.5-liter plastic bottles, whose dead soldiers were piling up in the kitchen.

"Say, Maman, if my eyes don't deceive me, you've packed on the pounds. I remember you used to look a little like Patrick Dewaere, but now you're more the Elton John type . . . Before you know it, you'll be dressing like Ben Chemoul! You haven't turned queer, have you?"

Yes, a nice guy at bottom, you might say. Full of tact and refinement. It was rare in their business. And on top of that always the first to pick up the check. Like in the good old Westerns, he almost always drew before his adversary, and the protests, and the alarmed little cries, made no difference. More often than not, all ended well: he footed the bill. A nut for the checkbook. A maniac for the ruinous signature. Sometimes you got the impression he had something to make up for. Maybe his assholery, maybe something less obvious, who knows? In any case, hats off! He paid for other people to put up with him. There weren't too many individuals who had such scruples. And besides, it wasn't really his fault if years of assistantship on idiotic TV shows had wound up making him a total moron. A few absurd images flitted through Maman's mind at top speed, like white birds tearing through a cloudy sky: Ettore Garofolo's death in Pasolini's *Mamma Roma*, the Roman suburb in July under the blinding sun, a photo of Jane Birkin in a TV magazine (she looked like a lost child, you wanted to adopt her), Legs Diamond collapsing under the rain outside a movie theater in one of Budd Boetticher's films, and a field of rapeseed in cinemascope, yellow as no one had ever seen anywhere except in Elia Kazan's films in the fifties. He suddenly wanted to see nature again, beautiful landscapes.

"Dear old Maman! Holy shit!"

Dagonard massaged his neck and groaned with pleasure, as if he were kneading a lump of bread dough. Then he dragged him to the bar, where he ordered two draft Heinekens. Maman avoided the bartender's gaze, but he couldn't help noticing him moving the hard-boiled eggs out of reach.

"Just one, Michel. I already had four earlier. I can't stop pissing. Must be the cold."

"What cold? What are you going on about? I've never seen such a gorgeous late November in Paris . . ."

"I don't know, I'm cold. Good Lord, do I get cold . . ."

Boxer placed his big mitts on Maman's face.

"It's true, you're freezing. Maybe you're coming down with something . . ."

He emptied his beer in one swallow and immediately ordered another. Maman had hardly wet his lips with his. He looked out at the street, blankly. The Opéra district was lost in the dark now, and he felt colder and colder. "This world is icy . . ." he thought, forcing himself to swallow another mouthful of beer. Dagonard was already on his third. That definitely wasn't going to calm him down. He belched loudly, which put a smile on his face.

"You know what you've caught, mother dear? I'll tell you what: myxomatosis! That's it, man. There are tons of cases of myxomatosis these days, at the gates of Paris. And now here it is, rampaging through the city. You're displaying all the symptoms: cold snout, bright eyes, chills, it's textbook. I'm sure of it. I studied to be a vet before I went into TV, you can trust me: myx-o-ma-tos-is."

Dagonard wept with laughter. His joke delighted him. Tears flowed into his beer. At least, as long as this was going on, he neglected to administer Maman big slaps on the back, which was something anyway. He spoke loudly so that everybody in the bar could enjoy his elephantesque finesse.

"MYX-O-MA-TOS-IS . . . Yes, my darling . . ."

Such familiarity was detestable—after all he had a first name, like everybody else, why did he spend his time ridiculing his last?—but Maman was dead set on enduring his ordeal to the end, without protest.

It had been so long since he'd had a REAL meal, with an appetizer, a main course, cheese, AND dessert, wine and service not included. Always damp sandwiches or cans of sardines opened in a rush at the corner of the table. With any luck, maybe he could even hit up Dagonard for a few hundred francs. That would compensate a little for the loss of income from the porno and let him keep his head above water for a while longer, perhaps even until the next booking. Because he would land a role soon, he was sure of it, in a film of importance, a film that would be selected for Cannes, and there he would win an acting prize, yes, he'd get back on track, and people would hear of him again, Georges Maman. His name would no longer be an object of derision. At forty-three, there was nothing he couldn't hope for. Plenty of great actors didn't begin their real careers until they were past forty, after all. He tried to think of their names, but Dagonard yanked him off his stool and dragged him out into the street.

"Come on, let's go, we'll grab a bite to eat like a couple of lovers. It's my treat."

For form's sake, Maman protested, but he didn't insist for long. Dagonard hadn't even asked him if he was free. His tact didn't go that far.

"I'd offer to take you to a good restaurant, but at the moment I'm a bit broke. We'll have to settle for the Drugstore Opéra."

Maman wasn't a big fan of that joint. The food was mediocre, and you were unceremoniously jostled by the crowd. But there or someplace else, what difference did it make, in the end? No matter where you went, you came up against the violence of the lights, the indifference of the people. Suddenly, he thought he saw Marie Beretta gesturing to him from across the street. She was wearing a blue coat, or maybe it was brown, in a style that seemed to him slightly out of date. From that distance, it wasn't at all easy to be sure of anything. At any rate, she looked like she wanted to speak to him. Did she have an urgent message to convey? He didn't have time to make up his mind. She'd already gone, not waiting for him to respond to her gesture. She was probably in a hurry. She was always in a hurry.

"You see, man, what I love about you is that you're always available to your friends. It's a rare trait, believe me."

Suddenly, Dagonard was emotional. He took the opportunity to give Maman a big slap on the back while

Maman looked anxiously to see if the light was turning red. At least, that's how it looked to Dagonard.

"Wait, but of course! If you've got myxomatosis, I've got to take it easy on you, my dear little mother. Word of honor: I'll stop thumping at you like a deaf man at a piano. Besides, you might be contagious, who knows?"

On the second pitcher of Beaujolais, Maman began to feel a little less sick. At any rate, he felt less cold.

"Do you remember Ma Barker?"

"Who the hell's Ma Barker?"

Dagonard imitated a burst of machine-gun fire.

"Bloody Mama."

This nickname came back to him hazily. To tell the truth, he'd completely forgotten it. People had made so many stupid jokes about his name that they all ran together . . .

"What about it?"

"You remember how we used to call you Bloody Mama, to make fun of you?

"No, I don't. In any case, I don't care, if you must know . . ."

Dagonard sprayed the room with an imaginary machine gun.

"No way you're going to tell me you've forgotten about Ma Barker! For Christ's sake, the gunslinger herself! With her sons, one of the great figures of 1930s American gangsterism, remember? Better than Bonnie

Parker and Clyde Barrow, better than Machine Gun Kelly or Legs Diamond, Bloody Mama! There's even a movie about her. Don Siegel, I think. No, Roger Corman, rather. Shit, I don't know anymore, I'll have to check. With Shelley Winters, in any case."

Dagonard stood. He picked up his machine gun decisively and fired several bursts at the crowd.

"Would you look at all these bastards! One's worse than the next! Ah! If I were John Dillinger! . . . TACTACTACTACTACTACTACTACTAC! The exit's that way! The whole world going down into the next one! Don't cry, I've got some for everybody!"

He sat back down and sponged at his forehead with a shred of paper napkin. He was brick red. Luckily there were neither dead nor wounded, nor even the least inkling of panic. To reassure Maman, he patted him affectionately on the shoulder:

"Yup! Mother dear, from time to time, one needs to do a little housekeeping. For us big shots, that's how it is. Look at Pierrot la Valise, Pierrot le Fou if you like, nobody stepped on his toes. A man needs air. A bit of space. Afterward, he feels at ease. You've always been too nice, always a little soft. That's how you wound up where you are, man. In this business, a guy's got to bite. Stab, sometimes! No mercy, all hands on deck! People would always say: That sweetheart Maman wouldn't hurt a fly. Bloody Mama's just a big milquetoast—that's what they'd say. Yeah, yeah. Stuff like that."

Try as Georges Maman might, he couldn't manage to chew his steak. Anyway, it was overcooked. And besides, he had bad teeth now. The teeth of an old man almost. The fries were dry, the salad wilted, burnt by the vinegar. Only the Beaujolais was right. That alone made it worth putting up with this jackass. Especially since there was still some hope of squeezing him for a few hundred francs, or maybe even a little more. Dagonard was always generous when he'd had too much to drink, and the next day, more often than not, he remembered nothing, which meant you didn't have to pay him back. Maman ordered another pitcher of Beaujolais.

"But it's on me this time . . ."

Dagonard almost flew off the handle and jerked the pitcher violently away.

"Out of the question!"

Best not to insist. He pulled out his machine gun a few more times and shot at random, in every direction . . .

"I almost lost my temper," said Dagonard, stroking Maman's cheek. He flinched.

For Christ's sake, really now, this guy was making him uncomfortable. He didn't like the way he was acting. If he hadn't been so broke, he wouldn't have let himself be held hostage a minute longer, he'd have walked out on him and his revolting meal and sprinted out into the street. The air in the drugstore was getting more and more unbreathable.

"You've got a bit of stubble, mother dear. But I like it."

JEAN-PIERRE MARTINET

Maman looked at the top of Dagonard's balding skull. He tried to hide his baldness by carefully combing forward a few flaxen hairs, but it did no good, all you noticed was his shiny pate, like a vaguely obscene billiard ball, hot and pulsing, you wanted to flick it and send it, just to see what would happen. But the lucky owner of this billiard ball didn't seem to realize he was being so unsparingly observed. He was content to ingest his chocolate mousse, gulping noisily. At least, as long as this was going on, he couldn't talk, which was something. The infuriating noise of the teaspoon scraping the bottom of the dish was easier to bear.

"This mousse is delicious. You going to finish yours?"

"No, I'm full. Have at it."

Boxer didn't need to be asked twice. With one big lick, the chocolate mousse was history. "He's going to start talking again," Maman, horrified, said to himself, "now that there's nothing left to devour, he's going to start talking. He's going to bring up every B movie ever made. Jacques Tourneur, Edgar G. Ulmer, Don Siegel, Joseph H. Lewis . . . He won't spare me a one. He'll recount *Gun Crazy* or *Out of the Past* frame by frame like he did last year on the phone for over an hour, and I'm going to die of boredom. Goddamn it! This guy's got me by the short hairs." Dagonard wiped his mouth with his hand and heaved a blissful sigh. Then he sat there in silence for a good long while, his eyes slightly lowered, as if suddenly the absence of chocolate mousse had plunged him into measureless sadness. Maman realized he was observing him, feigning nonchalance. He would do well to remember that Dagonard was cunning. And sneaky too. Watch out. Under the apparent buffoonery there was someone else. This way he had of looking at people "on the sly," as they said. Terrifying. He felt ice cold again.

"I disgust you, is that it?"

"Of course not. What are you talking about?"

"I do. I disgust you, I can feel it. I disgust everybody. Myself more than anyone . . ."

"Really, Michel . . ." Maman protested without conviction.

"You're such a hypocrite. No wonder you're an actor."

Dagonard's eyes were small, a bit piglike. Terribly mobile, too. They almost vanished into his face, overrun with fat. Once upon a time they must have been blue, but these days there was no telling their color. Try as he might, Maman couldn't manage it. As the disillusionments racked up, his eyes had lost their shine, they'd faded in the sun of the years, only a bitter gleam was left, slightly distraught, vaguely malicious, a curious mix of feigned bonhomie, frustration, and guile.

Maman said to himself that if he were a director, he would cast Dagonard in the role of Pavel Pavlovitch in *The Eternal Husband*. He really had the right physique.

"I'd like to be a little *more* of an actor, as a matter of fact. Since January, I've barely totaled a week's worth of work. Nothing but spear carrier stuff. I'm no longer even eligible for the Assédic. It's the pits, if you must know . . ."

All right, he'd taken the plunge. He felt a huge sense of relief. It was out. The call for help had been issued. Now the great solidarity movement just had to begin. Please and thanks, ladies and gents! Over here, help the Third World! Treat yourself to a brand-new pauper! Checks are accepted, as are all in-kind donations excluding old clothes, a person has his pride. Keep your old threads and send cash, it's urgent. Dagonard rested his hand lightly on Maman's and exerted a tender pressure. Maman did not withdraw his hand right away, but very slowly, almost imperceptibly, so as not to reveal too clearly how much this contact repulsed him. He made an effort to smile, as if he hadn't noticed anything. After all, it was no time to discourage goodwill.

"You know I saw *Wichita* again the day before yesterday at the Cinémathèque? It holds up pretty well. Not an ounce of fat on it."

"Oh yeah?"

Clearly, he hadn't managed to move Dagonard. Nothing to be done. The son of a bitch was still stuck in his old cinephile-rat reflexes. A desperate case. Yet he made another attempt:

"I even accepted a part in a porno, if you can imagine. Yes man. That's how low I've sunk. And the girl was so gross I couldn't even get a hard-on . . ."

Suddenly he asked himself why he was telling Dagonard all this. Probably the Beaujolais, he had no sense of decency anymore. Plus Dagonard didn't like women, so he felt a little less ridiculous.

"Yup! Couldn't get it up. I nearly died of shame. Can you imagine? In front of a crew! The next day I didn't go back. I stayed home in bed. Anyway, you won't catch me doing it again, I can tell you that. I'd rather kick the bucket."

This filthy story managed to bring a smile to Dagonard's face. Maman, you old devil! Stuff like that never happened to anybody but him! Nothing dismal was alien to him! He administered a few good slaps on the back to buck him up.

"Your first porno! That calls for a drink! Waiter, another pitcher of Beaujolais!"

Clearly, the situation was bleak. Maman had hoped that Dagonard might give him some advice on reorienting his career, maybe even offer him a part in a soap opera for a few months to make ends meet—after all, as an assistant director, he had a certain influence—but no, he found it funny, not the least bit shocking that a guy, who'd played Woyzeck when he was twenty-five at the Festival d'Avignon, to the universal acclaim of the critics of the day, should be reduced to dipping his wick in front of cameras to afford food. Normal stuff. Just a hoot. Nothing serious about it. Much less important than whether some Z-picture turnip nobody gives a shit about holds up thirty years later. At least he could have slipped him a few bills, discreetly, whispering in his ear: Listen, Maman darling, a guy like you, you shouldn't stoop to doing porno. Here's a little something to tide you over till things get better. No, no, no thanks necessary. I'd like to be able to do more. Go on, don't make a fuss, take it. Instead, all he thought about was stuffing his face, like a soldier on leave. He wallowed in his vulgarity with a slightly masochistic delight. Clearly, all the years that poor Dagonard had spent playing the high-class lackey on all the sets of France and Navarre had made him permanently soft in the head. What could he hope for now? He'd be an assistant until he reached retirement age. He'd been working on a film project for a decade, like everybody in the business, an adaptation of Jim Thompson's *The Nothing Man*, but the project was constantly getting delayed, to his great relief. At the last moment, a coproducer would pull out, or the guy he knew at Avance sur Recettes had just been replaced, or else the actors who'd been approached weren't available. The important thing was to have a project like everybody else. To go along at its tranquil pace, to fondle it, to keep on dolling it up. To grow old with it, without risk, without revolt, until the end. Yes, that was the important thing.

"I'm battling cancer, man, don't forget. For a decade now. I still have the right to claim extenuating circumstances, if you ask me."

Maman couldn't recall how Dagonard had come around to the subject of his cancer—by what tortuous conversational detours. He must have dozed off for a moment, more than likely.

"If you ask me."

Dagonard drummed his fingers on the table, staring straight at Maman. His tone was firm, almost aggressive. Anyway, it was a call to order. Best to tread lightly. Ever since he'd first gotten to know Dagonard, he'd been perfectly well aware how intractable he was when it came to his cancer. As intractable as he was when it came to Jacques Tourneur's films. No jokes allowed, and no suggesting that the cancer was just the fruit of his imagination, an alibi for marinating in mediocrity, like his *Nothing Man* that remained perpetually at a standstill. He'd even named it, the way they name hurricanes, or missiles: Yasujiro, pure and simple. Such an incorrigible cinephile. Yasujiro got around. Sometimes the liver, sometimes the larynx, sometimes the right lung. Or else he was generalized, on days of great despair. By virtue of talking about Yasujiro, Dagonard had wound up believing in him. He was his best friend, when all was said and done. He could always be relied on. As long as he was around, Dagonard would never be alone. One day, with any luck, he might even manage to give birth to a real cancer.

"That's right, your cancer, yes, how is it?" asked Maman without the slightest hint of conviction.

"We're fighting, my dear darling mother, we're fighting. But it's hard. God almighty it's hard!"

Dagonard was pleased. This imaginary battle gave him back a dignity he'd lost. He was no longer the pathetic assistant, the chrome dome, the piece of scum, the one who gets stuck with the grunt work and lets all the spit land right on his face without flinching when the winds are against him. He stood tall, machinegun in hand, like John Dillinger or Clyde Barrow.

"I'd rather we didn't talk about my cancer. Not tonight, if you don't mind."

"ok. We won't say another word about it. But I'll remind you that you're the one who brought it up."

Boxer didn't reply. Probably he was bothered by the way Maman had withdrawn his hand when he'd exerted that tender pressure. He must be ruminating his revenge. Probably that's why he absolutely insisted on toasting his guest's failure.

"You've never known how to fight, Maman, never. You only have yourself to blame. Basically, you're a loser."

"Thank you."

"Don't thank me. I'm not finished."

"Go on, for God's sake. Pretend you're at home."

"A loser *and* a creep."

"Is that right? Nothing else to add?"

"No, nothing. That'll do for tonight."

Georges Maman stood up abruptly, throwing his napkin on the table with a furious gesture he wanted to appear as theatrical as possible. He'd had it up to here with this psycho he hadn't even been able to squeeze for a few hundred-franc bills, just an utterly mediocre meal that would take him all night to digest.

"Bye now. You can go on yammering without me. Give my regards to Yasujiro."

Dagonard grabbed Maman by the shoulder and forced him back down. Then he gave him a big slap on the nape of the neck, roaring with laughter.

"Bloody Mama, you old devil, always so touchy! But you know I was only joking, right?"

"Is that right? You should've added subtitles."

"Come on, Ma, what've you done with your sense of humor? This aggressiveness of yours confirms my suspicions: You're coming down with a bad case of myxomatosis! First you're cold, you shake, then you bite, no doubt about it, you're displaying all the symptoms. Tomorrow I'll give you a ring and take you over to the vet. Let no man ever say that Dagonard abandoned old Maman in his time of need."

Maman observed that Boxer was getting more and more flushed. Eventually he'd be in such a state of inebriation, Maman told himself, it'd be a cinch to hit him up. Patience. But in the meantime, what an ordeal! Dagonard had taken hold of Maman's head and was squeezing it tight, the way you'd squeeze a grapefruit that's already been thoroughly juiced. His voice was meant to be reassuring.

"But your myxomatosis, Ma, you mustn't lose heart, you can pull through. Your eyes run, and your eyelids swell until they hide your eyes and stick together. Then the swelling reaches your lips, and your ears wither. I've heard your genitals tumefy too. But you're going to pull through, Ma. You're going to get through it, don't worry."

Jesus Christ, this guy had a real passion for rabbits. He should've finished his veterinary studies like a good boy and set up shop back home in the country, out in the Vendée, not far from the sea, instead of getting it in his head to go up to Paris and make it in the movie business. That's what had wrecked Dagonard. Maman couldn't help thinking that the poor kid had gotten off track, like him. Both of them had let themselves get caught in the trap, and every move they made to get out of it only mangled them further. He thought of that harrowing book about Hollywood extras by Horace McCoy, *I Should Have Stayed Home*. For crying out loud, the two of them should have stayed home too, chosen a cushy career, married a nice girl and had kids, like everybody else, instead of winding up here, on the far side of forty, getting plastered to try to forget they were nothing, absolutely nothing, total nonentities, life's castaways, whose calls for help went unheeded. Maman told himself he ought to have pity on Dagonard, that he and Dagonard were one and the same, and yet he couldn't summon up the slightest compassion. Just this obsession with the hundred-franc bills he needed so badly. He wondered with horror if he might not be capable of going so far as to kill for them. Nothing like a lack of money for you to demolish a man.

"You'll get through it, mother dearest. Don't cry. They've cured more hopeless cases than you. In the meantime, have a drink."

Dagonard poured his friend a generous cupful and ordered two calvados. Maman refused.

"Then two calvados for me, and another pitcher of Beaujolais for my friend!"

He pretended to protest, but it made no difference. "Anyway," Bloody Mama told himself, "I can make him drink that pitcher of Beaujolais easy, and with the two calvados, he'll be half out of his gourd. Then he'll have to cough it up." These TV guys never stopped complaining, but they were paid monthly, they had job security, and to top it off, they took themselves for artists, while he, Georges Maman, winner of the second-place prize at the conservatory twenty or so years back, who'd performed Shakespeare, Marlowe (he'd been a highly acclaimed Edward III), Büchner, not to mention important roles in movies and radio plays, was reduced to living by his wits, it really wasn't fair. Enough to make you scream with rage. No scruples, then. In a criminal society, etc.

"Really, Ma, in the old days you used to be more fun . . ."

JEAN-PIERRE MARTINET

"In the old days," Maman replied, bowing his head, "in the old days, it was different . . ."

Now all of a sudden he felt like blubbering. Must be the Beaujolais. Wine had always made him terribly sentimental. Whatever he did, he mustn't cry in front of Dagonard, he was just waiting for something like that to get the upper hand. But there you had it, nothing he could do, the tears trickled slowly down his cheeks, he tried hard not to sniffle, to preserve his dignity, he was blubbering for everyone to see. Odd to think there wasn't even a camera to film him. He was so natural, so affecting. It was so difficult to be natural in scenes like this . . .

"You're crying?"

Dagonard looked delighted. Finally, he'd found somebody more miserable than him. He took the opportunity to deal Maman a big slap on the back.

"They're such sentimental little beasties, ma'am . . ."

Then he added, swallowing his first calvados in one gulp: "Mind you, rabbits with myxomatosis always have runny eyes. The nose is generally obstructed by mucus. All quite normal then. Just go get the treatment, will you, first thing tomorrow. Promise me, darling, do you swear?"

This time Bloody Mama was on the verge of punching Boxer right in the face. He held himself back at the last moment. There was still the matter of the money.

"Listen, Dagonard, stop calling me 'darling.' And stop bugging me with this shit about rabbits. You're the only one who finds it funny, so give it a rest for Christ's sake."

The other man said nothing, settled for knocking back his second calvados. He called the waiter and asked for the check. Maman wondered if he hadn't been a little too hard on him. It would be pretty difficult now to put the bite on Boxer. Really, what a deplorable evening. Mercifully there was still a pitcher of Beaujolais. He filled Dagonard's glass to the brim. Dagonard emptied it in one gulp, making a sort of grimace, and held it out to him again, almost automatically, keeping his eyes down.

"Anyway, you still in love with Marie?"

The shock was rude. Maman flinched. He hadn't been expecting anything like this. He would rather Boxer have gone on rambling about rabbits, Jacques Tourneur, or his favorite gangsters, even his cancer if it made him happy, anything at all, but not this, not Marie, he had no right. He preferred to play dumb.

"Which Marie?"

"Marie Beretta, of course."

The bastard. He was perfectly well aware that he was hitting a nerve, even worse that he was throwing salt on a still open wound, which had never healed with the years.

"You're well aware that it's been over between me and Marie for ages."

JEAN-PIERRE MARTINET

"Sorry. I didn't mean to cause you any pain."

"But you haven't caused me any pain. That's all ancient history."

"Yes, yes, of course."

Dagonard poured himself another glass of Beaujolais. Bloody Mama studied him, furtively. No way to catch his eye. Like those of certain insects, his tiny organs of sight pried in every direction. He couldn't help thinking that whoever'd given him his nickname had been about as sharp as a marble. A boxer is loyal, it might leap at your throat to kill you or give you the greatest proof of its love, but it doesn't nibble at your heels for hours like a vulgar Dagonard.

"But in the booth, earlier, well, I mean when I was outside the phone booth, I had a curious, an indefinable impression that Marie was the person you were attempting to call."

"How's that? What are you talking about?" Maman stammered.

Dagonard avoided his gaze and went on in a calm voice, from which, bizarrely, all trace of drunkenness seemed to have disappeared.

"Yes. The way you got angry and hammered at the phone. It was her, I'm sure of it. Marie Beretta. You still love her. I mean, it isn't love anymore, it's something else, something that's been festering in your head. A sort of cancer, come to think of it. Like Yasujiro. And maybe it's all you've got left to live for, like me. But yours has a woman's name. A nice gun name too, Beretta, hell, you couldn't ask for a better one."

A jab straight to the heart. Maman was ko'd where he sat, which is no doubt slightly less painful than being ko'd where you stand, but certainly much more humiliating. He opened his mouth wide in search of a little air, like a fish dying on the sand, convulsing desperately. Dagonard added, almost in a whisper, still avoiding eye contact: "Marie made out pretty well in the end. Better than you. And yet she had a lot less talent. No fool, that woman. She spread her legs for Tranèze and then married him. And so Mother Beretta climbed to the top of the bill. And it doesn't matter in the slightest that, as an actress, she's more or less hopeless. Everybody acknowledges her talent nowadays, even the critics."

What, Maman wondered, was Dagonard driving at? Really, this guy was unpredictable, a genuine enigma. Sometimes he acted like a perfect idiot, sometimes, on the other hand, he seemed to be reading your mind, laying you bare with infallible intuition.

"You've seen her posing as a model mother in the women's magazines?"

"I don't often read women's magazines."

"Too bad. They're very instructive. There are Berettas on every page these days. Marie and her little Pascal. Full color in *Elle*, *Madame Figaro*, *Cosmopolitan*, I forget where else. The kid on his bike, on his father's shoulders, on a visit to Disneyland with his mother, holding Steven

Spielberg's hand in front of a giant photo of that horrible E.T. I'll be amazed if we don't have to see him at the White House, hopping up on Reagan's lap."

Dagonard was losing his temper. He was sweating profusely. He wiped himself with his napkin.

"I mean, come on. A whore like that. When I think of what she's done to you ... Believe me, mother dear, if you hadn't had that girl under your skin, you'd be the one at the top of the bill now, instead of driving yourself crazy trying to figure out how you're going to hit me up for a few hundred francs that you're never going to pay me back anyhow. Here, here's five hundred, and let's put it behind us."

Dagonard took a five-hundred-franc bill out of his pocket and slid it, with ostentatious discretion, under Maman's plate.

"No need to thank me."

Bloody Mama didn't say a thing, simply picked up the money, avoiding Boxer's gaze. He felt like an actor who realizes with horror that he's forgotten a crucial rejoinder and, incapable of improvising, just wants to get the hell out of there, away from the prying eyes of the crowd. The gap. Gaping. Obscene. At any rate, as soon as anyone mentioned Marie Beretta to him, he was effectively incapacitated. He couldn't say anything about her. The words stuck in his throat, formed a bolus that choked him. Good Lord, once again, he'd forgotten his lines. For opening night, it had gone well. It felt like the whole room was looking at him, waiting with bated breath to see if he could bring forth a single sound. The scraping of forks, the tinkling of glasses, the deafening conversations had stopped: Deathly silence. Utter disgrace. Why didn't they put out the lights, lower the curtain? What were they expecting from him, all these people who hadn't even paid for their seats to applaud him, but who, nevertheless, were turning out to be terribly demanding? They didn't shout, "We want our money back!," they didn't hiss, they didn't stomp the floor in a steady beat, they were satisfied to demand a reply that wasn't coming and would never come, no matter what, even if they stayed there, frozen like wax figures, for centuries and centuries. Suddenly Maman stood up and sprinted for the exit, bumping into several diners. He disappeared into a taxi and asked the driver to take him home, rue de Peupliers, in the thirteenth, by the shortest route possible.

When Bloody Mama woke up, the first thing he saw was Dagonard bending over him, shaking him savagely. He was talking in a gentle voice, full of solicitude, and yet Maman felt a sort of fear.

"Hey, Ma! Wake up! I hope you didn't do anything stupid! It's my fault. I should never have mentioned Marie. That's me for you. I've got no tact. A real pig. Everybody steers clear of me because of it. You will too, won't you, mother dear? You're going to shun me like the rest of them?"

How had he gotten in? Maman was quite sure he'd locked the door before throwing himself fully dressed on his bed and swallowing three Rohyphnols, which had immediately plunged him into a deep sleep. Surely Dagonard didn't have the ability to walk through walls, so how?

"You left your key in the door, so I let myself in. I rang the bell a few times, you know, but when nobody answered, I was afraid you'd done something stupid, is all. You left in such a hurry . . . Honestly, you scared the life out of me. At the drugstore, they thought somebody had been attacked, you should have seen the mayhem in the restaurant! As if you'd thrown a grenade before you left. Boom! The Palestinians! The ghosts of the Red Army Faction! Baader himself, come back from the land of the dead, and Ulrike Meinhof and the rest of them! Rise and shine!"

Maman's mouth was dry. Those fucking sleeping pills. Dagonard, the little lunatic, was having a grand old time imitating the sound of explosions. Whenever explosions and weapons came up, he was in heaven. That and rabbits, those were really his thing, much more than Jacques Tourneur or Joseph H. Lewis. Machinegun blasts! Mesrine! Bloody holdups! The extravaganza of terrorism! General meltdown!

"Say now, don't you have anything to drink?"

"Sure. There's still one bottle of Margnat in the kitchen."

"Plastic wine! Blech! Aren't you ashamed?"

"That's all I've got. If you don't like it, scram. I wanna sleep."

"Don't be cross, Ma," Dagonard said, heading for the kitchen, "we'll make do! When the going gets tough, the tough get going!"

Dagonard looked so happy not to be alone that he would have drunk anything, even bleach. Maman made some desperate efforts to revive himself, but they were not successful. A terrible desire to go back to sleep washed over him almost immediately. Like a grim Harry Langdon, he swung back and forth between two worlds. Nevertheless, he stood up. Whatever he did, he couldn't allow himself to fall back into bed. The floor was almost stable. The walls were walls, grimy but almost perpendicular to the almost stable floor. They weren't great at playing the role of walls but, apart from that, they were beyond reproach. Everything was ugly, therefore everything was real. It was just a bit skew-whiff, but he was used to that. He went into the bathroom and put his head under the spigot. Then he glanced at the alarm clock, which was at the bottom of the tub—really, he'd looked and looked for it, and he couldn't understand how it had ended up there, the goddamn alarm clock—and saw it was just past two. In the morning, no doubt.

The odds were fifty-fifty. He opted for morning, since it was night. "Holy shit," he grumbled, "pesky fucking Dagonard didn't waste any time tracking me down!" But he was resigned now, he knew that he couldn't get rid of him. No one ever got rid of Dagonard. Or else you had to be terribly strong, one of those "fighters" that the press praised in column after column, before which TV fell flat on its belly, and the people in power feared, evidently. The deciders! The France of winners! The ones invited to the Élysée! The rest of us were entitled to nothing. Just to make ends meet, and even that was too much. In serried ranks we advance, and quiet in the ranks! Sleep was a consolation, but Maman had a feeling it was a luxury he wouldn't be afforded anytime soon.

"My God, man, you've really been knocking them back lately! Say, that's a pretty swell photo of Lauren Bacall in your room ... What's that from? *Key Largo*? *The Big Sleep*?"

Dagonard's voice reached him from a long way off, as if he were at the other end of the world. Yet he was only a few meters away, the apartment was so small, a veritable prison. Maman had no memory of a photo of Lauren Bacall. Really, he couldn't imagine what he was referring to. Meanwhile, Boxer must be busy foraging in the Frigidaire, gorging himself on the cold leftover chicken he'd had delivered last week. And there was still one can of dog food. He hadn't had a dog in a very long time—to be exact, not since Marie Beretta had opted for a change of scene—but he went on buying the cans occasionally out of habit and ate them without complaint. It certainly wasn't any grosser than the goopy poultry-liver or duck-shit pâté they sold to humans; it was often much better, truth be told, and it aroused some strange nostalgia in him.

"Nice! Carrot-beef dog food!"

Dagonard was delighted. He must be on cloud nine. At least he hadn't gone out of his way to no purpose. At that very moment he was no doubt licking the can, risking laceration to the tongue. Boxer, you old devil! They broke the mold when they made you. He really liked him, when you got right down to it. Not a bad sort. Anyway, a guy who likes Jim Thompson and American B movies can't be fundamentally malicious, he was sure of it. Bloody Mama shot another glance at the alarm clock at the bottom of the tub, as if to say, "So you're still there, huh?"; then, resigned, or reassured (after all it hadn't replied, "And what's it to you?"), he went back into his living room-cum-bedroom, under the indifferent eye of Lauren Bacall.

"Where'd you get your poster?

Dagonard was standing in front of him, a slightly bovine look in his eyes, still licking his chops, the bottle of Margnat in his hand. He'd really gone to town on the carrot-beef dog food. Maman was happy for him. But that big photo of Lauren Bacall made him uneasy. He had no memory of pinning it to the wall, however much

he racked his brain it wasn't there. He'd never even re-
motely liked posters of actors. Frankly, he was too old
for it. He must have bought it one night when he was
sloshed, put it up above his bed without a thought, and
then, afterward, never paid it any further attention. At
any rate, it was a beautiful photo. Dagonard was right. A
beautiful photo of a marvelous girl, he wasn't ashamed
to have it in his place, far from it.

"Hey! Ma, you're not going to fall asleep on us now,
are you?"

Dagonard patted his face affectionately to keep him
awake.

"That photo there: *Key Largo* or *The Big Sleep*?"

"Honestly, I don't remember anymore," Maman
mumbled, running his hand unthinkingly through his
hair.

"*Dark Passage*, maybe?"

"Maybe. I don't remember."

Dagonard's prying eyes made him terribly uneasy.

"It's quite possible, in fact."

The way this guy's eyes could move was really incred-
ible. He noticed everything. Behind him. In front of him.
Around. Inside you. He might even be able to surmise if
you had holes in your socks or corns on your feet. Lauren
Bacall, for her part, looked you right in the face and you
lost yourself in her eyes, even if, at the same time, you
had the feeling she was a million miles away, transpar-
ent, perfectly indifferent to anything that might happen

to you in that moment. Bloody Mama didn't really have the strength to kick Dagonard out. Dagonard was much too strong for him, anyway. Not to mention the sleeping pills mixed with the alcohol had left him weak as a kid. All he wanted was to lie back down and sleep, sleep until the end of time. He stared long and hard into the eyes of Lauren Bacall, hoping that her magic gaze would soon whisk him off to dreamland, where you had to run very fast to stay put. But no, nothing doing, all he managed was to say to himself again: "But for Christ's sake where could I have bought this goddamn poster? And when?" He could cudgel his brains until the cows came home and never remember. It was almost like that moment in his life had been mysteriously stricken from his memory. He shrugged: "Bah, after all, who cares? I'm in deep enough shit as it is, I really don't see why I should torment myself over a trifle like this . . ." Dagonard had uncapped the bottle of Margnat and was standing in the middle of the room, drinking straight from it, greedily, as if he'd been on the wagon for a week.

"Not so disgusting after all, this plastic wine."

Timidly, Maman ventured, "Aren't you working tomorrow? Aren't you worried you'll be asleep on your feet?"

Dagonard waved his big mitt right in front of Bloody Mama's face, groaning like a bear that's just been disturbed during his siesta.

"Mind your own business!"

Best not to insist. A minefield—could go off at any moment.

"I've never been late to a shoot, mother dear, got it? In twenty years on the job! Dagonard's always on time. Always the first one on set! Even before the makeup artists! Yes, man. Once I was getting hammered all night with Maurice Ronet, and the next day I crawled onto set on my hands and knees, but I was there before anybody else. That's class, darling!"

Boxer's breath reeked of alcohol. Maman backed away discreetly. His only hope now was that he'd flop down on the floor dead drunk. Finally, he'd have some peace, he could sleep a few hours and Lauren Bacall could stop staring at him with her infuriating eyes, which were either sublime or tragically empty, no man could tell.

Dagonard wiped away a tear: "Ronet was a good guy, that's for sure. You could talk movies for hours with him, believe you me. Not like you, who never listens to a word I'm saying. It's rare to meet an actor who has something in his skull. Seventy-five percent of them are navel-gazing morons. And turn into monstrous pricks the moment they get successful. A lousy breed."

"Thank you," said Maman.

"Don't mention it," Dagonard replied, undaunted. "Anyway, you're different, you never made it big . . ."

"This fucking guy," Maman thought, "I could stab him in the throat with a pair of scissors." In fact, he had a magnificent pair with curved tips in the bathroom cabinet. Yes, that would have given him great pleasure, sticking him like a pig right there with a single thrust, no witnesses. The blood would have sprayed and splattered the walls, the rug, the poster of Lauren Bacall, but, afterward, how good it would have felt! He could take a long nap while he waited for the police, or sit around at his ease thinking up ways to get rid of the body, just as you might try to come up with the solution to a mid-level crossword, not exactly breaking your brain. Just thinking of Dagonard bellowing grotesquely as he gaped at his blood shooting like a geyser, Bloody Mama felt momentarily relieved, my goodness, almost happy. The demise of such an individual could not but gladden the heart and was even a sort of public health measure. With any luck, they'd give him the Légion d'honneur. His face spread into a smile.

"Are you smiling, Ma? That's goddamn good to see! I haven't seen you smile once all night. You can't imagine how it feels to see you relax a little. Mother dear, that calls for a drink! Red wine all around!"

Dagonard handed the bottle to Maman, who took a healthy swig, no bones about it. Since going back to sleep was out of the question, might as well gather strength for the night. The night would be long, it had Dagonard's face, Dagonard's corpulence, Dagonard's odor of sweat. Perhaps it would soon even have the odor of Dagonard's blood. And so Dagonard (because it was definitely Dagonard at issue here, no two ways about it), and so Dagonard, therefore, was very anxious to see the level of wine in the bottle getting dangerously low.

"Hey! Hey! Easy now! Don't forget your friends."

Boxer grabbed the bottle and set to suckling greedily. Maman reassured him: "I still have some reserves in the kitchen cabinet."

"You had me scared. I thought that was the last one."

He stopped drinking for a moment and asked Bloody Mama: "Do you think that, in profile, I look a little like Montgomery Clift before his accident?"

"Yeah, you're not wrong. A little bit . . ."

It was no time to contradict Dagonard. Best to acquiesce to all his ravings.

"Mind you, I don't have such nice eyes. No way. Eyes are important. You have no idea how much I'd like to have Montgomery Clift's eyes."

Maman felt a bit peckish all of a sudden. Probably that lousy plonk. He'd drunk too much too fast and was afraid he'd puke. In front of Lauren Bacall, that would have been awful. There was so much irony in those eyes. You sensed she was a girl who spoke her mind, yes, for sure, she wouldn't fail to tell you when you started acting like an idiot.

"Is there any dog food left in the kitchen?"

Now Dagonard was the one acting like he didn't hear. Maman shook him a bit, just to jostle a little sense into him. He told himself that if he brutalized him a little, maybe he'd forget about his murderous thoughts. After all, Boxer didn't deserve to be sent to the slaughterhouse, at least not right away. No one was perfect. So show a little indulgence, eh, Maman, ok? Maman nodded his head. Message received, loud and clear. He had no desire to be contrary. Not tonight. Tonight, he loved everybody. Even Dagonard. Good ole Dagonard! Always a laugh a minute!

"Dagonard, I'm talking to you!"

Clearly, the dog food was causing some problems. Dagonard was trying to conceal it. No easy task. All his limbs were trembling. He didn't like to answer a question when the question was no good.

"I'm talking to you, Dagonard!"

Bloody Mama was becoming more and more vicious. Dagonard was shrinking before his eyes, like in Tex Avery's cartoons, but it was a lot less funny. No one was laughing. It was even kind of creepy, truth be told.

"What dog food?"

"The carrot-beef. There was only the one can."

"Oh yeah?"

"Yeah. Nothing left to eat."

Dagonard had shrunk so much in the wash that his voice seemed to be issuing from nowhere. Maman had the impression that Lauren Bacall's lips were moving, quite gently, with the utmost primness. He recognized her slightly husky voice. There was no mistaking it. It was definitely her. That girl had charm to beat the band, any man would go to the ends of the earth with her. For her eyes alone, for her voice alone. And for the rest of her too, of course.

"Nothing left to eat, honey?"

She had a way of pronouncing *honey* that made you melt toot sweet. There was no resisting it. She seemed to be teasing you and, at the same time, inviting you on the most marvelous journey imaginable. Anyway, it was a far cry from Dagonard.

"I ate the whole can. Maman. I didn't realize. First-rate."

He started licking his chops again.

"Rabbit-flavor Whiskas I knew about, my cats are crazy for it. But wow! First-rate!"

He couldn't get over it. It was even better than a meal at Bocuse. Strange to think that because of this moron he no longer had anything in the fridge! Into the doghouse with you, Dagonard! Down, Dagonard! Heel! But he was pulling himself together again, the animal. He was growing before his eyes. He was turning vicious. Much more vicious than a boxer. In a pinch, a person could get along with a boxer. More like a bear, a vicious grizzly! Any minute now he might turn into one of the extinct species, one of the monstrous beasts! The pterodactyls! The brontosauruses! The iguanodons! All that! . . . The giant rats that ate film strips! The worst! The triceratopses ready to charge at anything resembling a filmography! To rip to shreds anyone who has the gall to prefer Buñuel to Edgar G. Ulmer! "Ugh! The dirty beast!" Maman said to himself, staring at Dagonard. Playing host to a fifteen-meter film-consuming T-Rex! That was all he needed. It really wasn't nice having that in your house. All of a sudden Lauren Bacall stopped talking. Her lips were sealed. Irritating, like background noise.

"I brought you some pretty pictures, Ma."

Dagonard tossed a handful of magazines on the bed. Bloody Mama thought they were porno mags but, very quickly, as soon as he saw the unwholesome gleam in Boxer's eyes, fleeting though it was, he understood that they were something else.

"Yes, some beautiful engravings."

"What makes you think I'd give a shit about engravings at this time of night? Why don't you do me a favor and let me sleep?"

"I bought them specially for you at the drugstore. Beautiful color photos of Marie Beretta. Also little Pascal. And Tranèze, of course. The whole Holy Family. Just pure happiness on glossy paper. Like, look here: Tranèze directing his old lady, perched on a crane, eyes glued to the camera. What a show he puts on! Coppola's modest by comparison!"

Maman feigned a casual glance at the magazines and stretched, yawning conspicuously. But inside he was seething. It was no longer a matter of gathering strength. He had more than enough.

"Listen, my dear Dagonard, you've got to get out of here now. Take your magazines and off you go, nice and quiet. I don't give a shit about Marie Beretta. Get that through your skull, and the rest of you too. I don't want to hear any more about any of it."

Lauren Bacall gave him a complicitous wink. "Well played," she seemed to be saying. "Well played, George." Maman lunged at Dagonard. He wanted to strangle him, truth be told, more than he wanted to chuck him out like a common thug, but he settled for trying to nudge him toward the exit. No easy thing. Dagonard put up a fight. He wouldn't budge. He seemed bolted to the floor. The fucker had taken root. He was absolutely committed to taking the game into overtime. He was a boulder, Boxer was, with all his muscles tensed, tetanized, no way he was going to get out of there. Where he was, he intended to stay. Bloody Mama turned around to face Lauren Bacall, studying her eyes for the slightest sign of encouragement, but no, nothing. She was content to stare mysteriously, half drugged Mona Lisa, half Mrs. Magoo, groping blindly through a world of which she only caught hazy glimpses. That was the way with women. They encouraged you to take risks, they demanded the best of you, and at the last moment, when you needed them most, they were gone, they ditched you like an old sock. Better off with Dagonard, in the end. At least he was in no hurry to leave you.

"Another glass of red, Dago old pal?"

Maman's smile was a bit forced, but, if you weren't too picky, it was fine. Dagonard was OK with it and moaned with pleasure.

"I wouldn't say no, Ma. But after that, you'll take a look at the pretty pictures. Promise?"

"Promise."

He went into the kitchen to look for another bottle of Margnat grand cru classé. When he came back and uncapped it in front of Dagonard, he shot another glance at Lauren Bacall, just to see if she didn't feel the least bit bad for ditching him, but no, it was final. Final. Like Marie. Exactly like Marie. He tried not to break down in tears. Forever. Gone forever. Permanently. And now this idiot who wanted to force him to look at photographs of her! But what the hell was going through his skull?

"Look at this and tell me it isn't a crying shame, ten color pages dedicated to this nobody! Her projects! Don't you have projects too? Her secrets for staying young! And this, listen: 'Only Tranèze knows how to shoot me!' Of course, he's the only one who's *going* to shoot her . . . She's so bad no one else wants to hire her! Even Sophie Marceau has some genius by comparison!"

Maman almost shot back that, be that as it may, in the last few years, Marie Beretta had played several lead roles for directors other than Tranèze, but he preferred to keep his mouth shut, since Dagonard would have only taken it as an opportunity to twist the knife. The hardest to endure weren't the photos of Marie, or the photos of Tranèze, but the photos of the kid. The filthy little curly-headed angel! He couldn't stand him, with his rich boy eyes, a little brat the whole world had smiled at from the day he was born. At any rate, ever since Marie had decided not to keep the child she'd been expecting with Maman, a long, long time ago now, he'd taken a dislike to kids (and it was after that that their relationship had started to deteriorate, the whole thing going south at breakneck speed).

"Mind you, there's no denying Marie's beauty. She looks more and more like Carole Laure ... Still like a teenager ..."

Dagonard was lost in admiration. Bloody Mama wondered for a moment if he, too, wasn't a little in love with Marie Beretta, but the idea struck him as so outlandish he burst out laughing.

"What are you laughing about?"

"I don't know. Honestly, I don't know ..."

"It's not that funny ...

"No, not that funny at all."

"Anyway, you're acting weird. You don't seem to care at all."

"Actually, I don't care at all."

"All's not lost, in any case. You're going to get back on track, man ..."

"Who told you I wanted to get back on track? Are you getting back on track?"

Dagonard lowered his eyes and whispered in a hoarse voice, in which he tried to put as much emotion as possible: "Oh, you know, if it weren't for this fucking cancer, I'd have been as famous as Tranèze ages ago . . ."

Lauren Bacall, up there on the wall, looked like she could hardly contain her laughter. Clearly, she didn't take Dagonard's cancer seriously—not even a little. Yasujiro didn't impress her one bit. But then nothing impressed her, she had guts, that girl, she could even give you complexes, poor men.

"Yeah, man, instead of being a TV flunky, I'd have won an Oscar in Hollywood a long time ago, believe me. And *The Nothing Man* would be playing at the Cinémathèque, not on the pathetic little movie screen in my skull!"

Boxer's face pushed up close to Maman, who instinctively flinched.

"You know that guy, Tranèze, never had any clue how to work with actors. Never. A pretentious nobody is what he is! Hawks wouldn't have even taken him on as his third assistant! Back then, they knew what a director was . . . He was a guy who had to blow everything up, mother dear! Hurl a grenade on the whole shebang! No more Tranèze! No more Marie Beretta! No more horrible curly-headed brat! No more glossies! No more movies! Bam! No more TV! Les Buttes-Chaumont in smithereens! The blast to end all blasts!"

Having exhausted the charms of explosives, Dagonard switched over to the machine gun. TACTAC-TACTACTAC. Best to take cover, he was blasting away in every direction. Only Lauren Bacall kept her cool. It was slightly embarrassing to feel so jittery in front of such a beautiful woman, but, tough luck, what would be left of Maman if it weren't for humiliation? Happily, it didn't take long for the machinegun to jam and a soothing calm to fall upon the room. Boxer wiped his face, dripping with sweat, then downed the rest of the bottle of wine.

"I'm tired, mother dear. I think I'm going to head home. Your lousy plonk has done a number on my stomach."

Dagonard looked suddenly devastated. As if he'd aged a decade. He rubbed his stomach morosely.

"You've given me heartburn with that vinegar of yours, Ma. Not a nice thing to do to an old friend."

"You want me to call a taxi?"

Boxer didn't reply. He looked as if he weren't there at all.

"A taxi, how do you like that? TA-XI. Vroom, vroom. And, afterward, beddy-bye. Bedtime for Dagonard. To-morrow's another day. Maybe, anyway. It's not a *sure* thing. We shall see."

The ex-future great director suddenly started sob-bing. It was the final flourish. How low would he sink?

"I should have stayed home for sure. Been a vet like my papa, that's what I should have done, mother dear. Make an honest living, be of use, out in the fresh air. I've only ever liked animals, really, especially rabbits. Rabbits are nice, innocent. A good goddamn trade, being a vet. My God, if I could turn back time . . ."

Dagonard couldn't hold back his tears any longer. His head was filled with images of the countryside, the landscapes of his childhood, it was all coming back to him in bursts.

"Did you know rabbits have intestines three meters long, mother dear?"

"I know, Dagonard, I know."

"And that in summertime a lactating rabbit can drink up to four liters of water a day?"

"I know, Dagonard, I know."

"Groundsel, poppy, milkweed, cabbage, fumitory, clover, alfalfa, dandelion—do you know those words too, Ma?"

"I know them, Dagonard, I know them. Yes."

Dagonard fell silent and headed for the door. Suddenly Maman was no longer so eager to see him go. All things considered, the night hadn't been half bad. It had just left him with a slightly lukewarm feeling, like everything in life.

"Don't bother calling a taxi. I'll walk home. And on my hind legs at that. Don't worry about me, it'll be all right."

Boxer gave him a half smile.

"You can keep the pretty pictures. I bought them specially for you. Now you'll always be able to jack off to photos of Marie Beretta. G'night."

Before closing the door behind him, he poked his head in again and murmured in a funny voice:

"Oh, right! I forgot. That's a nice little toy you have in the fridge; but watch out. It's not for amateurs."

The door slammed and Dagonard disappeared down the staircase. Bloody Mama wondered what he meant. What toy could he be talking about? He was startled from his reflections by a muffled noise from the stairwell, the sound of a body falling and tumbling down the steps at full tilt. He rushed out to the landing.

"Dagonard! No broken bones?"

"What the fuck! Fucking staircase!"

Dagonard was lying on the third-floor landing, in the position of a prone gunman.

"Why didn't you take the elevator?"

In the moment, it didn't occur to Ma how outlandish this question was. With great effort, Boxer got back on his feet and dusted himself off, twitching like a madman. His flabby mouth twisted in every direction, but he couldn't make a sound. Maybe he was trying to explain that he hadn't taken the elevator because, quite simply, there was no elevator. At least he hadn't boarded the stairs! Dagonard stood there looking like Stan Laurel when he was about to burst out sobbing and the whole audience is already dying with laughter, Maman thought. Except in this case, frankly, it wasn't funny enough to make anyone double, or quadruple, over. He was even starting to feel pretty goddamn anxious. And to top it off, the elevator had flown the coop! The pincers clamped down again on his neck, without warning. He had no choice but to ask himself the terrifying, unignorable question at last: Would he ever manage to get rid of this kook? Was he condemned to be saddled with him his whole life long, to the last breath? The prospect wasn't exactly thrilling. The implausible truth: They were Siamese twins. Thanks very much. Joined together forever. The mysterious, obscene membrane. He shivered with horror at the thought. For the moment, the mysterious disappearance of the elevator faded into the background.

"Dagonard, answer me. What's wrong? Can you speak?"

He hadn't broken anything, which was something. After all, if he could walk, he just had to get out. He'd persecuted him enough for one evening. The night was half over now, a foul November night, wet and cold, and all this time wasted for a mere five hundred francs and a mediocre meal, without even a grand cru classé! Being a loyal and devoted friend, and indulgent into the bargain, got you nowhere. Five hundred francs. A pittance. Really it was a small price to pay. Maman said to himself, "That fucker ought to pay five hundred francs an hour, minimum, for people to put up with him. Otherwise the gentleman's just got to go it alone. Unfortunately, he can't stand being alone. Therefore: He has to pay the piper, no buts about it!"

"Are you sick, dear old Dago?"

(In his head, Bloody Mama was doing the math. Dagonard had imposed his presence on him for at least eight hours. At the union rate, he owed him close to four or five thousand francs, but he wasn't greedy.)

The other man really looked like his bell had been rung. Maman was afraid for a moment that he'd lost what little mind he had left. If he was going to throw him out, it was now or never. The lights were on a timer, and when he pressed the switch, he could see that in the course of his tumble Boxer had lost his checkbook, his papers, and a wad of brand-new two-hundred-franc bills. The magnificent Montesquieu! Seeing them gave him fresh strength and courage: crisp and shiny, not yet soiled by contact with unclean fingers. As lovely and hypnotic as if they'd been made by counterfeiters. There must be twenty or more of them. It wasn't a fortune, but it would be enough to keep him going for a while.

"You lost your papers and your checkbook, Michel. And some cash too. Lucky I noticed it . . ."

Dagonard emitted a groan no doubt meant as a thank you, while Maman diligently tucked the lost items back into the inside pocket of his jacket.

"There you go. But be careful next time, old man. I'll help you down to the street and put you in a taxi. Watch out when you pay him. They can spot a drunk guy from a mile off. I speak from experience, believe me. Remember where you live?"

Boxer was looking none too steady on his feet. He knew he hung his hat someplace, but where? The world was so vast. Paris consisted of thousands of streets and hundreds of thousands of apartments, but which one was his in this great big mess? He had no idea anymore. Bloody Mama took his friend by the shoulder and helped him down the last three flights.

"You're going to be fine, old man, just fine. Don't you worry."

Ma had tears in his eyes. He felt perfectly at ease in the role of the old friend who's always around whenever anybody needs him. Manly friendship. Because it was he, because it was I.[5] John Wayne and Dean Martin in *Rio Bravo*. Yes, that's the way it was, and almost as beautiful, they were just lacking Howard Hawks's direction. But he wasn't available at the moment. John Ford either. Henry Hathaway might have done the trick, but, tough luck, he was unavailable too. Raoul Walsh was incommunicado. Jacques Tourneur, AWOL. A real graveyard. It was one hell of a November, rotten weather, not the slightest glimmer of hope anywhere, a man might have felt awfully alone if not for the fond friendship of a Dagonard to warm the heart.

"That's it, old man. The fresh air will do you good." Slowly, he withdrew the arm that was keeping Dagonard upright to test whether Boxer could stand on his hind legs unassisted. OK, not too shabby. A slight swaying to and fro, but nothing too serious, his range of motion remained feeble, despite the glacial breeze that had begun to blow in punishing gusts down rue des Peupliers.

"There's a taxi, old man. Wave him down. At this hour, it's utterly miraculous."

Dagonard waved his hand without conviction in the direction of the car, which drove past without stopping.

"Shit, missed him."

Maman was relieved to observe that Dagonard had recovered the use of his tongue. So the shock hadn't been as violent as all that. Maybe in the long run, with any luck, it might even do his poor brain some good. Anyway, he was getting cold as a stone. This awful wind was a bone-freezer. Bloody Mama was sorely tempted to leave Boxer standing there and go crashing into his bed, once he'd downed another dose of Rohypnol just to calm his nerves, but he preferred to make sure he was getting rid of the hulking old slob first. After all, even if he couldn't remember his address, the taxi could still take him spinning in circles around Paris until the crack of dawn, if only to relieve him of those last two-hundred-franc bills, then dump him out on the sidewalk of an unknown street. The horrible thing would be if Dagonard asked the driver to take him back to rue des Peupliers, to Maman's place, but no danger of that, for the time being he probably wasn't capable of remembering this address either.

"It ain't warm, Ma . . ."

Boxer looked at Bloody Mama pleadingly:

"Don't you think we might be better off going back upstairs?"

Maman pretended not to hear. Desperately, he scanned the dark streets, hoping to spot the headlamps and dome light of a taxi.

"Mother dear, tell me that in profile I look a little like Montgomery Clift . . . Say it . . ."

"Of course, of course you do . . ."

"You've got to do better than that! Once more, with feeling . . ."

Boxer was turning vicious again. His hands reached out for Maman's neck, and Maman took a quick step backward. And what if Dagonard strangled him then and there, without witnesses, then took off running? Bloody Mama believed he was perfectly capable of it. Best to grin and bear it.

"It's true, you do look like him . . . Really it's an amazing resemblance . . ."

Dagonard dropped his arms to his sides. He seemed suddenly calmer. But it didn't last.

"Still and all, Ma, what a nutty idea, stashing a lovely thing like that in the fridge!"

Now he was back onto that again. Maman wondered anxiously what he could be referring to. He could hardly stop himself from dashing back up the stairs, rushing into the kitchen, and opening the fridge. There were so many things he didn't understand tonight: the poster of Lauren Bacall he had absolutely no memory of pinning to the wall, the alarm clock in the bathtub, the elevator that had flown the coop without warning—a rough day, truth be told. And now, to top it all off, this strange object Boxer kept claiming to have found in his fridge! As if he weren't already between jobs and short of cash . . . Dagonard must've had something to do with it. The guy had a gift for fucking up everything in his vicinity the moment he arrived. Maman regretted not having pinched more money from him. He should've stuck the whole wad straight into his pocket without the slightest hesitation. As usual, he'd lacked nerve. It was a bit too late now to rectify the situation, but never mind. He'd do better next time, if there was a next time, because he'd made up his mind never to see this walking calamity again.

"Here's one! Don't miss him this time! And keep an eye on his driving, don't be a sucker!"

Maman rushed at the taxi and nearly got himself run over. Waving his hands around wildly, he forced the driver to a stop. Then he opened the door and sent Dagonard unceremoniously flying into the back seat. Good riddance. See ya later, and the later the better. Boxer didn't take offense. He never took offense, even when somebody wasn't convinced that he looked like Montgomery Clift. He cranked down the window and looked Bloody Mama straight in the eyes for once, giving him a faint, ironic smile. He looked perfectly lucid, as if he were suddenly completely sober, or as if, up to then, he'd just been putting on an act in rather poor taste.

"Still, be careful, mother dear . . . You never know . . . Accidents can happen anytime . . ."

His tone was saccharine, almost cloying, full of innuendos, vaguely malicious allusions, creepy threats. On certain words it grew as shrill as that of a hysterical, and perfectly horrifying, little girl. Still smiling, Dagonard waved goodbye with his right hand, and the taxi pulled away. Maman watched it disappear down the end of rue des Peupliers, and waited for a while to make sure it wouldn't just circle the block. Mercifully, it didn't reappear. Yet Mama didn't feel even the least bit relieved. Far from it. If anything, he felt even more anxious now that Dagonard was gone.

And still no elevator. Elevator gone. In the wind. Eight flights to climb! Of course nobody in the building had mentioned it to him. They all despised him, that was clear. Worse: They ignored him. A failed actor elicited nothing but indifference. They scarcely said hello back when they used to glimpse him in a walk-on role in a soap opera, and even now there wasn't one of them who could put a name to the face. Jacques Legras? Erich von Stroheim? Fernandel? Who knows? Anyway, nobody gives a shit. Tomorrow, Maman told himself, I'll call the landlord and lay into him. There's only so much disrespect one can take. Tomorrow. Yes. They'd see what he was made of. After all, tomorrow or in a few days, there was no point getting upset, people tended to take these sorts of things seriously. Especially when you were six months behind on your rent. Best to keep your mouth shut. Bill collectors, he had to admit, were the only ones who still took an interest in him. Those folks adored him, clearly: pink paper, blue paper, yellow paper, final notice before action, summons before seizure, legal letters written with love, there was nothing too lovely for him. He had no idea how to respond to such heartfelt outpourings, but he felt a little less alone, at any rate, surrounded by such warm affection. Of course, no one could remove an elevator like that, in the dead of night, the way they might cart off a grand piano or a gas stove, but was that any reason to get tied up in knots? There was no end of strange goings-on under the sun. One elevator more or less was no reason to move heaven and earth. Right? Of course not. Or of course. Anyway, that wasn't the problem. The problem, for the moment, the question, was: What's in the fridge? What mystery toy? What unbelievable gadget? What sordid trinket? Maman was expecting the worst. For example: a late-model atom bomb, the portable kind; or the pope giving his Urbi et Orbi blessing even though nobody had asked him, especially this time of night. It might equally well be Jean-Luc Godard and Robert Bresson dancing the tango mournfully in an ascetic blockbuster directed by Andrei Tarkovsky. Why not? So many strange things could be hidden behind the enamel door of a workaday Frigidaire, he was ready for anything. Perhaps he'd merely discover a deep-frozen version of Marie Beretta in a take-out tray, ready to eat? Or else nothing, just an empty fridge, hopelessly snoring with nothing within, just empty cans of dog food, moldy dregs of beer, an old piece of rock-hard camembert? Anything was possible. But the important thing right now was to reach the top floor. Bloody Mama found that it was a feat almost as great as the ascent of the Annapurna by the north face (or south? he couldn't quite remember, and anyway he couldn't care less; he'd always hated mountain climbing and mountain climbers; let them hang from their ropes against the snow and blue sky; let them stop poisoning the poor world with their idiotic exploits). In short, it was no piece of cake. Nor was opening the door once he was up there, nor not trembling as he tried to put the key in the lock (the emotion was violent, the heart pounded a bit). On entering his apartment, Maman felt a slight sense of shame. He almost asked if there was anyone home. He so hated to barge in on anybody. He felt a little like you do in a hotel room that you absolutely have to check out of by noon. Truth be told, he'd never felt truly at home anywhere, except perhaps on the stage in a theater when he'd been up-and-coming. Woyzeck, Edward II: he felt like he existed. Back then, maybe, in those faraway times, the place was habitable: a stage. But now . . .

JEAN-PIERRE MARTINET

"Anybody here?"

He scratched his throat. It was a bit idiotic to give in to the uncontrollable urge to make sure there was no one else in the apartment. He'd tried to resist, but no, nothing doing, he'd caved.

"Anyone?"

His voice was bizarre. He hardly recognized it. It wasn't his, at any rate. Sounded more like Bourvil. That was it for sure. Yes, the voice of dear old Bourvil. Slightly quavering, with unpredictable high notes. It was rather reassuring, when you got right down to it. Nobody more reassuring than dear old Bourvil. In any case, it was awfully well imitated, no two ways about it.

"Yoo-hoo . . . Anyone?"

Hilarious. A sure-fire laugh. He'd missed out on a good career as an impressionist, among other things. But what hadn't he missed out on in his life? Especially since nowadays impressionists were terribly unpopular. He ought to give it some thought. Not idiotic, when you got right down to it, as far as fresh starts go. Especially since he had never really felt like himself. Who was he, when you got right down to it? Well into his forties, he didn't know the first thing about himself. Always abstracted, with his head in the clouds. As a stop-gap solution, there was no question it was better than porn. Rather than performing Büchner or Racine, he'd imitate Bourvil, Funès, or Georges Marchais, big deal, the difference wasn't so vast. He knew the bit from *L'Eau ferrugineuse*,

for example, by heart. It was a good bit, a fine professional routine, just a little out of date, but who cared?

"*L'eau ferrugineuse . . . L'eau ferru . . .*"

He couldn't remember what came next. A bad start
in the business. He chuckled nervously.

"*L'eau ferrugineuse . . .*"

Best to begin from the beginning. Whatever you do,
don't panic.

"*L'eau féjuri . . . L'eau ferrugi . . .*"

Hats off. It had been quite a while since he'd heard
such a good impression. All that was missing was the be-
ret pulled down over his ears. To twist around. But no
one was laughing, apart from him. There wasn't much of
anyone around. Truth be told, it was even rather chilling.
Especially since he'd forgotten the rest of the sketch.

"*. . féfé . . fénuri . . fériju . . .*"

Nobody was laughing, he had to admit it. There
were nights like that, when the audience was just bad.
And then of course the actors aren't as good. They overdo it, trying to shake all those people dozing in their
seat, but nothing doing, now nothing's happening on
stage but grimaces and gesticulations, words repeated
and repeated until gradually you're overcome by an urge
to vomit, and an uncontrollable desire to take refuge
backstage.

"Dagonard? Hey, hey! Dagonard! You there?"

As a question, it was frankly idiotic, Maman was
well aware. He called himself a moron, but doing so gave

him only a moment's comfort. With a guy like that, you never know. He was quite capable of secreting himself in a corner of the apartment while you were sure he was miles away.

"Dagonard. Dagonard darling..."

His voice was slightly more assured. He left off imitating Bourvil since it amused no one, not even him (on the contrary, it scared the bejesus out of him). After conducting a thorough exploration of the apartment, he had to admit that Boxer really was gone. He wasn't hidden in a corner of the scenery like those mysterious personages in picture puzzles you find by turning the page around and around. The magazines he'd bought were still on the bed, in the exact spot where Maman had tossed them. An empty plastic bottle lay on the floor, alongside the remnants of the dog food. In short, everything was in order. Just the usual horror, Bloody Mama told himself, carefully sidestepping the bottle, because for a long time now he'd detested the noise that plastic makes in its death throes, it put his nerves on edge, he wasn't sure why. And anyway, first things first, there was that fridge to visit. He had to make up his mind. He couldn't go back to bed before he checked. He was expecting the worst. What could Dagonard have been talking about? To screw up his courage, he was going to uncap another bottle of wine in the kitchen. He was very close to the fridge now. Never had its snoring sounded so creepy. Hoping to butter it up, he gave it a little slap on the right side. The fridge moaned with pleasure, but even that wasn't reassuring. He suddenly remembered the Dutch girl slashed into strips by Sagawa the Japanese student. Hopefully he wasn't going to make a discovery like that! Escalopes of human flesh on cardboard plates! Now there was something he wouldn't recover from. But no, it couldn't be anything as horrible as that, because Dagonard, a dreadful coward, would have fainted. Fridges were sites of death in any case, he'd always been certain of that. Freezers too, come to think of it, people killed themselves in them, hid dismembered bodies—in short, nothing very decent. Maman knocked at the fridge door before making up his mind to open it. If he was going to do it, best do it properly. One never knew. He announced himself in a very confident voice: "It is I, Maman."

It was he, no reason to be alarmed in there, for the love of God, it was he and no one else, no need to make such a fuss, each to his own, every man for himself, he had no intention of bothering anybody, take it easy in there.

"Hey, hey! Don't panic, whatever you do! Otherwise I'll lose it . . ."

There he was, getting all hot and bothered. He realized he was acting preposterously, but he was determined to stand firm. At any rate, Ma wasn't so easily impressed. He'd seen others. He repeated himself to screw up his courage: "It's true, I've seen others." But other whats? To this, he was quite incapable of formulating an answer and his anxiety became acute. He downed half the bottle of red wine. As a result, his thoughts seemed less silly, the ready-made expressions less stupid. He even recognized he'd shown a certain amount of talent. Of course, in the old days, he'd often been given better lines to deliver, but the years had gone by and now he had to write his own. Marie. Marie. Maybe it was Marie. Why not, after all? What a funny path, all the same . . . A miniature Marie model he could keep at home. Just for himself. A miniature not suitable for adults. He'd be content with that, and how! He'd never felt like an adult anyway, so . . . Suddenly he wondered if he wasn't as drunk as Dagonard had been when he tumbled down the stairs. Maybe not quite as drunk, but close. "You're endangering your health," Marie Beretta always used to tell him, even way back then. She wasn't wrong, he was already drinking a fair bit, especially before he went on stage or answered questions on camera (he couldn't help it, it scared the living hell out of him). Anyway, something was always being endangered. Marie Beretta never went overboard. Watched her weight. Not an ounce of fat. Not a suicidal bone in her body. Managed what money she had. One eye on the bottom line, the other on her waistline. Career first. Bitch. The bitch. Narcissistic. Monstrously egocentric. And no talent whatsoever, Dagonard was right about that. None whatsoever. Dagonard had flair. A goddamn connoisseur. Life hadn't been kind to him, no, you could say that again, no kinder than it had been to Bloody Mama. He wondered how he could have let such a nice guy go. Just thinking about it brought tears to his eyes. He clenched his fists to keep from crying. If Dagonard had been a woman, even an ugly woman, even a cripple, he'd have asked her to marry him immediately, yes, because really, he was an amazing person, Dagonard. Really, they were made for each other, they were so alike. Could there ever be a lonelier couple? Dagonard? A lord, like him. Both of them were of the race of lords, it didn't even bear discussion. And he'd as good as thrown him out! He'd robbed him! Not even Gobineau could have imagined such a kingly son! Bloody Mama banged his head against the fridge over and over, very violently, to punish himself for his disloyal behavior. He wound up gashing his forehead, and the blood streamed down onto his face. He was flooded with a sense of well-being. It helped him get himself together, a little. He regretted getting slightly carried away. Still. Had to keep his head. Or what was left of it. What little. Keep it safe. But it was so refreshing. He didn't even feel the burn. Yet the shame remained. Because, after all, Dagonard wasn't rolling in it, and maybe he was having a hard time making ends meet like everybody else. How much does an assistant director on a TV show bring in? However much he racked his brains, he couldn't calculate. No clue. Anyway, he didn't care. When you're broke, everybody's overpaid; minimum-wage workers seem like billionaires, the air becomes unbreathable. The air was becoming unbreathable. It was because of Marie Beretta. Every time he thought of her, he choked. It was a pain he couldn't describe. Even a genius writer like Chandler or McCoy would have thrown in the towel. Anyway, who was asking him to describe this pain? Only sleep. Only sleep consoled him. Or maybe death, who knows? Where was the continental divide?

"How stupid can I be . . ."

Hearing his own voice reassured Maman somewhat. He felt that he was going to find the strength to open the door at last. It was him speaking, no doubt about it. No one but him would tremble like this, performing the most innocuous gestures.

"A total freak."

No voice rose to contradict him. There was no murmur from the back of the room. It was a bit vexing, of course, but, basically, normal and reassuring. There you go: normal and reassuring. The world was full of normal and reassuring. Full of normal and reassuring people. That's how it was and it was pretty damn good. Life was pretty good if you didn't look too closely. Yes, but there you go, what if you looked at it TOO CLOSELY? It wasn't a bad question, Maman was forced to admit, even if his heart wasn't really in it. He almost thanked whoever had asked it but, since he was the one who'd asked it, he stopped short. Because, finally, if you looked too closely, what did you see? You had to face the facts: it was a revolver. Bloody Mama reached out and touched the gun with his hand, stroking it gently. The ice-cold feel of it did not displease him. Really it was a beautiful object. It even occurred to him that he hadn't seen anything so beautiful for a long time. Not a revolver, as he'd first thought, but a Beretta model 92F semi-automatic pistol. Despite the blood running down his face and slowly obscuring his vision, he managed to read the letters inscribed on the gun. For a moment he stood there ecstatic before the name engraved on the grip, at the center of a magic circle: M. BERETTA. By what mysterious path had this pistol fetched up in his Frigidaire? He didn't even formulate the question. Deep down, he didn't care. Now that the initial fear had passed, he felt almost relieved. Was that all it was? He was familiar with weapons, had handled them on sets. And since death had been brought to him on a platter, why be choosy? At any rate, he no longer had any desire to wait and see how his story would end. The movie no longer interested him. In fact, he'd never really interested himself. He caressed his face with the pistol. An extremely gentle caress. The pleasure it gave him was so violent he almost wanted to scream. He checked that the weapon was fully loaded, then lowered the safety lever. He murmured, "We apologize for this momentary interruption of the picture," which set off a fit of giggles he had a hard time mastering. When he'd calmed down, he put the barrel to his temple.

AT THE BACK OF THE COURTYARD
ON THE RIGHT

My opportunities for absorption were not extraordinary. I was therefore continually sick at heart. At the back of the courtyard and to the right.

Henri Calet

La Belle Lurette [Ages ago]

Some days, in summer, when the air is so muggy, the sky is so dirty, despite the blue horribly masquerading as childhood, some days, yes, with Calet's novels in your pockets, like stones for when you jump into the water, and the rustle of foliage in your heart, you take a small step back. Ages ago. Once upon. Different times. You remember. You were born. "A small heap of soft flesh." You're already afraid, but still, it's childhood. No brilliant thing, childhood, not too pretty, but what about adulthood? Fiancées are cold. Despite appearances, the elevated metro near La Motte-Picquet runs a little slower each day. It gets increasingly difficult to find anyone to play belote with. You end up playing in front of a mirror, all by your lonesome. Ricard helps a little. Pork butchers get murdered. Where do the florists live? No one remembers. Gigantic black holes. Ages and ages. You're nothing but a prewar product. Ugly. You're born a larva, between poop and urine, and you depart a drooling crab, backward and with a few legs missing. But you'll have seen it through. Pride cometh from coming full circle. "Suicide? What for?" asks Calet, at the end of *Monsieur Paul*. "For in the final analysis, all that's left are corpses. No, don't overdo it." The important thing is knowing how to wait. No moaning, no pointless weeping. Night comes again. You knew it would. You didn't come out on top, but oh well. You didn't even figure out how to live. You had a good laugh, in spite of it all. You remember. The misery. The humiliation. The fetuses piling up under the city walls. The grimy mornings and the turds in the sanitary buckets. Your mother: abortionist, whore, and, on occasion, fortune teller, and last but not least: Madame Caca. Tenderly beloved, though. You fuck on the fly, joylessly, in vacant lots, under the sad eyes of little brothers. Behind the walls, you engage in a poor imitation of life. Days wasted. Irredeemable loss. "Days wasted repeating what has been done before. Better is always possible. From sunrise to sunset, never knowing what the sun has to do with it." A nasty story, really. Rather sad.

JEAN-PIERRE MARTINET

Right from the start. This isn't Proust. The past doesn't prettify anything. Communion girls don't dream of Christ. Little tossers. This is the ungrateful age. "They all jack themselves off." The director's son ejaculates in your mouth. Your mom gets fucked a few feet away from you, not out of depravity but for lack of space. "A bad start." You're living in "a steam room, a dump, a cathouse. A brief stop on the journey from life to death." The past won't pass. "More prisons than bowers" (Yves Martin). Not many young girls in bloom but distressing little sluts with dubious panties. They still keep your heart warm in the darkest hours of the night. They've all died in the hospital, the little lovers. Poor workers: straight from the spinning mill to the morgue, and who gives them a thought?

Ernestine went into the hospital. From the spinning mill to the hospital, that's the real circuit.

A case of syphilis like hers was rare. After each injection, the flesh of her thighs, her buttocks, came off in fist-sized chunks. She grew all rotten and purple.

She lost her long brown hair. She died in the hospital, the beautiful whore.

And I could no longer look at her and see her all friendly and white and perfumed. I could no longer fuck her with my eyes.

Thin, stained shirts, a lacey bra blue at the underarms from sweat, jersey panties with stains inside, along the seam ... dirty laundry I'd pick up and sniff to find the smells that bring on erections.

Everything that didn't smell good was good for me.

Strange spring in the morgue. Calet, after several suicide attempts, figures out that, in spite of everything, you've got to live. "Either you must do something, or something must be done to you," says Herman Melville in "Bartleby." You had a few laughs, even so. You've been a man, or tried to be. You've choked back your tears in silence, hot and salty. You weren't very well armed for life, more of a caterpillar, more of a slug to start with, but what the hell, you fought like everybody else. You pretended to believe. And like everybody else: bad son, bad brother, bad lover, bad father. Bad everything. It's only as a corpse that you play your part pretty well, and even then, it remains to be seen.

Henri Calet: his darkness, his dignity.

Now that beneath the bowers the light grows dim.

Odilia weeps, but not with any particular pain. The rings around her eyes widen a bit. Tiny little purplish pockets.

The storm finally moves off from Burrth.

Ward Waterwind lets himself slip into the water without a cry.

Mes Couilles[1] crawls across the floor on all fours in great pain. He's hammering imaginary nails. He used to work for the Gas Company. Now he complains he hears the sea in his ears.

One rainy day, Monsieur Antoine lights out to somewhere far away. "His dripping, bloated body was fished out at the dam, between Suresnes and Puteaux." He never even saw the blue hole in the clouds.

"Goodbye, Ma'am!"

The day of death is no worse than any other.

The most important thing is that the john is white, clean. Some nice diarrhea, then clean it all up, without panicking.

Until the end of time, the blood will be flowing from Odilia's vagina.

Poor life. Poor lives. Calet only ever spoke about the humble, like Dabit, like Guilloux, like Bernanos. He loved those who are passing through, those who are about to die and who know it, and are pretending not to know it, and put on sweaters and underpants and brush their teeth, shit, go to work, come home, fuck, go to bed, whatever the weather, shit, fuck again, sleep, don't sleep, and at the end of the day start weeping in silence, because after all, as children, they dreamed all the same of another life, because after all, yes, it has to be said, they did dream of another life.

Calet said it. Fucking life.

Because this isn't the way it should have been.

In spite of it all, how beautiful the stay was. You still remember.

"In Suresnes sometimes we ate mussels and french fries and drank rosé. In shirtsleeves, under the arbors."

How beautiful the years were. And all those women's heartbreaking bodies you held tight against you.

"This is my youth and I have no other."

You had only this poor little life. It's better than nothing. When you're Madame Caca's son, you can't be too picky.

A few of Calet's heirs: Yves Martin, Jean Eustache, Maurice Pialat, Georges Perros.

You've seen women's muffs in full light. Nowadays it's a bit darker. You've licked, you've been sucked, and then you've gone back to die alone, in your room, in a heap of old newspapers and empty bottles.

But that stay: fabulous.

You still remember it.

Yes.

Like everyone else, washed, combed, and wiped, I went my filthy little way, under the city in the eight-thirty convoy of salesmen, saleswomen, accountants, and typists routed toward the piles of madapolam and the additions of the Ledger.

You breathed in the scent of women and their cheap manufactured perfumes.

You cleaned your teeth with a corner of the ticket, or your ears with your fingers.

Little girls with dirty necks were reading greasy books, books that had made the rounds. A healthy serving of printed love in the musty tunnels, far from the sourness of family.

A beautiful stay, truly. A beautiful trip.

Francis Ponge: "Unsociable, lugubrious, profoundly ruined from the inside out, Henri Calet is the darkest writer I know, with a darkness to match Lautréamont or Lucretius."

He knew where he was going, Henri Calet.

A longtime Communist, in the end he got used to living without hope.

Nothing but death.

"Goodbye, Ma'am!"

Henri Calet knew.

Now, different times.

You fret a little more than you used to, but nothing to brag about.

Ages and ages since life was any fun.

Never really knowing what the sun has to do with it.

Fiancées are cold.

At La Motte-Picquet, every other metro transports corpses.

A gloomy Sunday for next Thursday.

[Text published in *Subjectif* no. 4, November 1978.]

NOTES

WITH THEIR HEARTS IN THEIR BOOTS

1. *Le Hérisson* is a light-hearted satirical weekly printed on green paper, "the color of optimism," according to the publisher.

2. "J'ai la mémoire qui flanche" ("My memory is going") is a song written by Serge Rezvani and first recorded by Jeanne Moreau in 1963.

3. The Sainte-Anne hospital near the Glacière metro stop has long specialized in psychological and addiction problems.

4. Assédic (short for "Association pour l'emploi dans l'industrie et le commerce") was an agency that collected and paid unemployment insurance contributions.

5. Montaigne's "Of Friendship" (trans. Donald Frame): "If you press me to tell why I loved him, I feel that this cannot be expressed, except by answering: Because it was he, because it was I."

1. A character in Henri Calet's *La Belle Lurette* whose name means "My Balls."

William Boyle is the author of eight works of fiction set in the southern Brooklyn neighborhood where he was born and raised: *Gravesend*, which was nominated for the Grand Prix de Littérature Policière in France and shortlisted for the John Creasey (New Blood) Dagger in the UK; *Death Don't Have No Mercy*, a story collection; *Everything Is Broken*, published initially in France and subsequently serialized in *Southwest Review*; *The Lonely Witness*, which was nominated for the Hammett Prize and the Grand Prix de Littérature Policière; *A Friend Is a Gift You Give Yourself*, winner of the Prix Transfuge du meilleur polar étranger in France and an Amazon Best Book of 2019; *City of Margins*, a *Washington Post* Best Thriller and Mystery Book of 2020; *Shoot the Moonlight Out*, listed by CrimeReads as one of the ten best noir novels of 2021 and nominated for the Grand Prix de Littérature Policière in 2023; and, most recently, *Saint of the Narrows Street* (coming from Soho Crime in February 2025). He currently lives in Oxford, Mississippi.

Alex Andriesse is a writer and an associate editor at New York Review Books. He has translated, among other books, Roberto Bazlen's *Notes Without a Text*, François-René de Chateaubriand's *Memoirs from Beyond the Grave*, and Marcel Schwob's *Spicilège* (published by Wakefield Press).